THE BILLIONAIRE'S CHRISTMAS CONTRACT

A CLEAN SMALL TOWN ROMANCE

CHRISTMAS BILLIONAIRES

BOOK THREE

LAURA HALEY-MCNEIL

HUERFANO PRESS, LLC

Huerfano Press, LLC

P. O. Box 874

Littleton, CO. 80160

Laura Haley-McNeil.

The Billionaire's Christmas Contract: Christmas Billionaire Series, Book 3

Huerfano Press, LLC

For Indy

CONTENTS

CHAPTER 1

*L*eah Rendell parked her parents' van filled with four teenaged boys in front of the Mardale, Colorado, second-hand store. On this Friday after Thanksgiving Day, she gripped the steering wheel and took a deep breath. She wouldn't let her broken engagement spoil the holiday celebrations.

"Hey, guys, let's do some shopping and remember, we're buying clothes you can wear to church." Forcing a smile, Leah looked over the back of her seat into the dark eyes of the foster boys her parents were raising on their ranch. Taking the boys shopping was the distraction she needed from the last few months when she juggled wedding planner appointments with the English literature classes she taught at an east coast college.

Those wedding plans crumbled to dust when the day the quarter ended, she walked into her fiancé's law office and realized Charlie was doing more than preparing court cases with his assistant.

Shell-shocked, wounded and unable to speak, Leah could only stare at the blanching couple. Then she did the only thing she had the strength to do—she placed her engagement ring on Charlie's book-case and stepped back into the law firm's paneled hallway.

Now, Leah sat in the van and swallowed the emotion welling in her throat. The boys shifted in their seats and stared out the van's windows, clearly eager to stretch their legs and explore a town smaller than their inner-city neighborhoods.

Except Zeke. The distrust in the eyes of the boy who had arrived at the Rendell Ranch for Boys last night showed he was plotting his escape to the Denver neighborhood he'd called home until his mother had disappeared.

"We're going into Tara's Shoppe," Leah said, her voice steadier than she felt. "You can pick out a shirt, a pair of pants, and a pair of shoes, then we'll head over to Danielle's bakeshop for a treat. Deal?" She pressed the button that opened the van's doors.

Frankie, Harry and Carl cheered and tumbled out of the van.

"Yippee," Zeke said, his voice flat. He stepped out of the van and into a puddle.

Water sprayed back into the van, over the curb and against a powerfully built man striding down the sidewalk, a cell phone pressed to his ear. The man froze, his gaze dropping to the pants and tweed jacket now dripping with muddy water.

Zeke's eyes widened. The fear in his paling face made Leah's heart squeeze tight. The other boys went rigid, their mouths open in stunned surprise.

"I'm so sorry." Leah leaped from the van and raced to the man. She lifted her hands to him, not sure if she should brush the grimy droplets off his pristine apparel or stand back and grimace. "Don't worry. I can take care of this." She was talking too fast, and she couldn't stop staring at the trickles streaming down his clothes.

The man murmured something into his phone, then slipped it into his pocket. His crystal blue gaze settled on her before dropping to the jacket that probably cost more than most people made in a month. Muddy rivulets flowed down an outfit that had obviously been tailor-made for his well-toned physique.

"It's fine." The corner of his mouth curved.

For a moment, Leah caught something familiar about the man. Did she know him? He wasn't from Mardale. Though for the past ten years, she'd only visited during the holidays, she still knew everyone in town, and she'd never seen him. He dressed like someone planning to spend the weekend on his multi-million dollar yacht.

"No, it isn't, and I can fix it," she said. From the corner of her eye, she glimpsed a panicky Zeke backing away.

Leah snatched the boy's hand and gently tugged him toward her. She felt his resistance, but her insistent pull brought him next to her and face-to-face with this stranger and his mud splattered clothes.

She looked at Zeke and arched a brow. He gave her that what-do-you-want-me-to-do look she'd seen on several boys' faces when they first arrived at the ranch. If they played dumb, maybe the problem would go away. She pressed her lips together and tipped her head toward the man.

"You owe Mr.—" Leah's breath caught in her throat. Who was this man? She gave him an apologetic look. "I'm sorry, I don't know your name."

The man's surprised look turned to amusement. "Bryg Winslow."

"Well, Mr. Winslow, this is Zeke." She looked at the teen. "What do you say to Mr.—" She stopped and shifted her gaze back to Bryg. "As in Bryg Winslow the ..."

She glanced at the boys, who watched intently. Zeke's eyes widened, waiting for her to finish. Several townsfolk murmured Christmas greetings, their gazes flicking from Leah to Bryg as they passed.

Was this Bryg Winslow the founder of the Winslow empire? Though she hadn't followed the media stories about the handsome billionaire who always had a beautiful woman on his arm, she'd seen enough pictures to recognize him. What was he doing in Mardale?

"Bryg is fine." He smiled, his gaze resting on her in a way that was distinctly disconcerting.

Her jaw worked, but no words came. She was staring at Bryg Winslow and realizing he was better looking than any photo of him she'd seen, and he looked pretty good in those pictures ... along with his date *du jour*.

Her mouth slammed shut, and she looked at Zeke. "What do you say to Bryg?"

"Sorry," Zeke murmured. He shifted his eyes to Leah. "Who is he? How come everyone's staring at him?"

Leah glanced around and saw the sidewalk was more crowded than she'd ever seen it, even at Christmastime.

"Let's just leave it with the apology," Leah said. If Bryg wanted the boys to know who he was, *he* could tell them. "Now all of you go into Tara's and pick out your clothes."

The boys rushed toward the store. Zeke followed slowly, but continued to glance back at Bryg.

"I'll be there in a minute," Leah called after them, then turned to Bryg. Her gaze dropped to the now drying spots. "I'm so sorry this happened. I can take care of stains. I have a great recipe for removing grime. Your clothes will look as good as new."

"As much as I appreciate the offer, cleaning won't do any good. I'll just throw them out." His mouth tipped in a smile that made Leah's heart drum like a marching band.

"You can't throw away perfectly good clothes," she said, his cavalier comment shocking her. She knew several people who would appreciate owning the designer threads.

"I'll take care of the clothes, but thanks for the offer." He turned away, then looked back at her. "Since you know my name, I think it only fair that I know yours."

"Leah Rendell." She gave a nervous laugh, then winced. This wasn't high school.

"It's nice to meet you," he said, and he did seem glad. A slight frown creased his forehead. "Any relation to Mayor Vern Rendell and his wife Mavis?"

"They're my parents." She blinked. How did Bryg Winslow know them?

"Then you're familiar with the Rendell Ranch."

"I should be. I was raised there." Mostly raised there. The Rendells had adopted her when she was two. She might still live at the ranch if she hadn't been awarded a scholarship to the east coast college where she now taught.

"Then maybe I'll see you this afternoon, when I meet with your parents," Bryg said. He gave her a direct look.

"You're coming to the ranch?" she stammered. She went cold with shock. Her parents hadn't told her, though they'd been busy preparing for the Thanksgiving holiday. If she hadn't been trying to recover from her broken engagement, she may have realized they hadn't said much.

"I take it you don't live in Mardale anymore," Bryg said.

"No," she said, the homesickness she felt whenever she left Mardale tumbled through her stomach. "I live back east now, but I'm home because …" Because her fiancé was a cheat, and she had to call off her wedding. "… because the college where I teach takes winter break between Thanksgiving and Christmas. I always help out at the ranch during the holidays." Her heart ached. If she hadn't caught Charlie with his assistant, they would've shared their vows this Christmas Eve.

"Which college is that?" Bryg lifted a brow. He seemed interested.

"Braxton College. It's a small college."

"Yes, I know," he said with a grin that made him more handsome. "Their English department is renowned. That's quite an impressive school."

"I enjoy it," Leah said, and felt deep color creep into her face. At least she'd enjoyed teaching at Braxton until … she'd let that part go. Her gaze dropped to Bryg's jacket. "If you change your mind about having your clothes cleaned …"

"I'll let you know," he said with a smile. "It was nice to meet you, Leah Rendell." He held out his hand.

Leah extended hers and felt cool strength in his firm grasp. He said something else, but she was too flustered to understand. His cell phone rang, and he released her hand, sending her hand into a void that made her long for his touch.

"Sorry." Something flickered in his eyes and his mouth tipped. He slipped the phone from his pocket and glanced at the screen. "I have to take this, but I look forward to seeing you again. Soon." Turning away, he pressed the phone to his ear and strode down the sidewalk.

She watched him climb into a luxury SUV and drive away. Even after it turned the corner, she still stared down the street.

Why was Bryg Winslow meeting with her parents, and why hadn't they told her?

Several townsfolk passed Leah and wished her a Merry Christmas. Leah pulled her gaze away from Main Street and returned the greeting. She took a deep breath. She would not think about Bryg Winslow, but she had to think about why her parents were meeting with him.

"Leah?" Frankie, the tallest of the foster boys, leaned through the store doorway. "I got my clothes." He opened the door a little wider and proudly showed her the orange and purple striped pants. The shirt's flowing sleeves were long enough for his lean arms. He extended one foot covered with a sparkly shoe.

"Wow, you look great." Leah stepped into the store. "How are the other boys doing?"

Frankie lifted a shoulder and stared down at his new clothes. "Can you take a picture of me to send to my friends?" He gave her a hopeful look.

"I'd be glad to." Leah dug her phone from her purse and snapped pictures of all the boys, something even Zeke didn't seem to mind. "Now go change and bring me your new clothes so I can pay for them."

The boys brought Leah their clothes and thanked her. She was grateful she could buy them clothes. These boys had struggled enough during their brief lives. She'd do whatever she could to help them follow the right track.

She set the outfits on the counter and handed Tara her credit card.

"I see you were talking to that Bryg Winslow." Tara rang up the purchases and slipped the clothes into a shopping bag. "I suppose you heard."

That made Leah's heart stop. "Heard what?"

"Holly Johnson put her ranch on the market," Tara said. "She's been talking about doing that since Oliver passed."

"She'd mentioned she was thinking of selling," Leah said slowly. She'd talked to Holly when she'd brought the boys to church for the

Christmas pageant rehearsal. She felt sad when Holly said someone was interested in buying her ranch.

Tara arched a brow at Leah.

"Bryg Winslow wants to buy Holly's ranch?" Leah asked, numb with confusion. "Why would he want a ranch in Mardale?" He was Bryg Winslow. She'd read he owned homes all over the world, including a thoroughbred farm in Kentucky. That had to be much nicer than a rough and tumble ranch in Mardale.

The bell above the shop door rang and a couple with three children stepped into the shop.

Tara's eyes widened. "You need to ask your daddy about that," she said, and stepped around the counter to greet the family.

"Come on, guys." Leah suddenly felt tired. What business had her parents been discussing with Bryg? "Let's go to the bakeshop." She pulled the shopping bag from the counter and led the boys out of the store. "We can get a snack before we return to the ranch."

The boys cheered and dashed across the street, except Zeke. His hands in his pockets, he sauntered, and Leah wondered if he would stay at the ranch. The muscles in her stomach tightened. Her parents had raised hard-hearted boys before, but none seemed as remote as Zeke.

"Remember to look before crossing the street," Leah shouted after the boys, but by then they had slipped into the bakery.

Leah's mind raced back to her conversation with Tara and the news that Bryg Winslow was interested in buying the Johnson ranch. A lump rose in her throat. A billionaire wouldn't be interested in a ranch in Mardale without a purpose in mind. She felt vaguely uncomfortable. When she returned to the ranch, she'd ask her parents why Bryg was coming to the ranch.

And she'd ask them why they'd said nothing to her.

CHAPTER 2

*B*ryg guided the luxury SUV to the home he'd rented while he scouted Mardale and the surrounding countryside. He wouldn't be here if his front team had successfully negotiated contracts with the ranchers. When Bryg had asked his staff about their progress, they'd said one man stood in their way—Mayor Vern Rendell. The other ranchers in the area wouldn't sell until they talked to the mayor.

Bryg told the team to return to New York. *He'd* talk to the mayor. A muscle worked in his jaw. There was nothing he liked more than a challenge.

He'd spent a couple of days driving around town and through the countryside, meeting people, discussing his plans, then he called the mayor. Vern had said he didn't think they had much to discuss, but agreed to meet with Bryg. He had invited Bryg for Thanksgiving dinner, but Bryg always spent that day with Adam and Cheryl Moore, the foster parents who had welcomed him into their home when he was twelve years old. He had thought it the worst day of his short life. It turned out to be the best.

This afternoon, Bryg would drive to the Rendell Ranch and

present the plans his development company had created. He had no doubt Vern would like his ideas.

His employees had consulted with several manufacturing companies who wanted to move their plants to a small town near a big city but needed tax incentives for the jobs they'd bring to the area. Mardale, Colorado, would be the perfect place. It was in the country, and it was close to Denver.

Until three months ago, Bryg had never heard of Mardale, but when his scout team brought him the data for the area, he knew he'd found the perfect place. What had struck him were the views. The friendly townsfolk provided the pristine setting to raise a family. Sadly, the town's population was aging. The children who had been raised here went to college and never came back.

Bryg's throat felt tight. If he'd been raised in a town like Mardale, he never would've left. Pushing that thought from his mind, he sped down the country road and gazed at the snow covered meadows. Already, he could see the homes with families enjoying fresh air and sunshine. When he'd shared his ideas with the landowners, many had resisted, but he knew these old ranchers had no one to inherit their land. They had to sell, and he'd offer them more than the appraised values.

He felt pleased with what he could do for these people. The retiring ranchers would win, the families moving to the area would win. The companies opening their new manufacturing plants would bring in the revenue that would make Mardale a thriving town again. Under Bryg's guidance, his staff had created the perfect plan.

He had made several offers to the ranchers. Though they wanted to discuss their decisions with the mayor, they did seem interested in Bryg's proposals.

Vern Rendell had been reticent, but he'd agreed to meet with Bryg today and discuss the benefits of having corporations build plants in the area.

Bryg's mouth tightened. The Rendell ranch was the most beautiful in the valley with the river flowing through its meadows, and its gently rolling hills. Now Bryg had met the mayor's daughter.

The willowy woman with dark brown hair and golden eyes aroused an emotion in Bryg he'd never felt before. The air in his lungs stilled. He couldn't gauge his feelings because what seized his stomach when he met Leah was far too unnerving.

In the distance, he saw the home he'd rented, and released his breath slowly. He'd flown to Colorado to revitalize a community. He wouldn't let a woman distract him. Once his staff had forwarded the proposals for the ranches to him, he'd schedule meetings with the ranchers so they'd understand how selling their land to him would benefit them and the community.

The familiar energy he felt when he was about to close a deal rushed through him. He couldn't wait to make these offers to the locals, and he couldn't wait to change Mardale from a dying town to a revitalized community.

He turned into the rental house driveway and guided the SUV into the garage. Inside, he strode to the master bedroom and shrugged out of the ruined jacket and pants. He tossed them to a corner. He had appreciated Leah's offer to clean the clothes, but he didn't need them ——a far cry from his struggling childhood. Even when he lived with the Moores, his life had been modest.

Though he sometimes yearned for those days, they disappeared when a major corporation bought the company he'd started in his dorm room. With that came the changes including the Milanese fashion designer who flew to Bryg's New York penthouse once a month. Bryg always had his assistant order several sets of each style he selected. Sacrificing these clothes was a small price to pay if it meant buying the Rendell ranch. Once the mayor agreed to sell his ranch, the other landowners would do the same.

Bryg climbed into the shower and let the water stream through his hair. This morning, he'd met the woman whose image hadn't left his mind since she'd looked at him. In her eyes pulsed apology, and not recognition, which was a refreshing change. Most women he met were more interested in what he could do for their careers.

Having his clothes splattered was a sacrifice he was glad to make if it meant seeing Leah again. With any luck, he would this afternoon. Maybe he'd bring the stained clothes with him. If anything, she could clean the clothes well enough so someone else could wear them.

An emptiness rolled through him. He regretted he wouldn't be in town long enough to get to know her, but he had a business to run. Once he had the signed contracts, there'd be no reason for him to stay.

In his mind rose Leah's smiling face, and his heart quickened sharply, because in that instant he knew leaving this town would be harder than he'd ever thought possible.

WHEN LEAH and the boys returned to the ranch, the boys showed Leah's parents the clothes they'd bought. Though Zeke tried to hide his excitement, his eyes shone with the pleasure of having something new to wear.

After lunch, Leah helped the boys clean the kitchen, then she and her parents made sure the boys were settled in their rooms and understood their homework.

Leah followed her parents into the living room and told them she'd met Bryg Winslow.

"He said he's coming here this afternoon to meet with you." Leah looked from her father to her mother. She didn't miss the cautious look in her parents' eyes.

"He is," her father said on an exhaled breath. "He has plans for this area. I told him I'd hear him out."

"Plans? As in buying the ranches around here?" A hint of panic stirred in Leah's chest. Tara had said Bryg would buy the Johnson ranch.

Her father looked at her, his mouth tipping ruefully.

"Will you sell him the ranch?" Leah forced calmness into her voice.

She hadn't lived here in ten years, though she loved visiting her parents and returned whenever she could. This Christmas vacation had given her respite from her broken engagement. She released her breath slowly. She'd never thought her parents might want to sell the place.

"I can't answer that until I know his plans." Her father's eyes held the reluctance of making this decision. "But we won't do anything until these boys have been raised. Join us in the meeting. I'd like to hear what you think."

She could already tell him what she thought, but she nodded and went upstairs to her room to change. She'd been stunned when Tara told her Bryg's plans for the area. Why hadn't her parents said anything?

Her second thought made her still. Maybe her parents were ready to sell. They weren't the young couple who had bought this ranch thirty-five years ago. Because they couldn't have children, they'd adopted Leah's brother David. Four years later, they adopted Leah. Her parents' desire to raise children never waned, and over the years they opened their hearts and their home to boys in need of guidance.

Leah slipped into a sweater and a pair of slacks that had been her favorite outfit when she taught. The clothes were comfortable and looked nice, though they couldn't compare to the clothes Bryg Winslow had worn this afternoon.

She flushed deeply. She wished Zeke hadn't stepped into the puddle and splashed Bryg, but Zeke was a boy and a mischievous one. When he'd confessed to Leah's parents what he did, their surprised looks seemed to make Zeke wish he'd been more careful. Relief flooded Leah. Maybe Zeke wasn't as hard-hearted as he pretended to be.

Leah wished Bryg had allowed her to clean the jacket and pants. Then he could wear them again, but being a billionaire, he'd have a magnificent wardrobe. He wouldn't miss the clothes he'd worn today.

Sitting at her vanity, Leah ran a brush through her hair. Her cell phone rang, and she glanced at the screen, at Charlie's name wavering in big, white letters. She'd been here four days, and now he was calling her? If he could wait to call her when *he* was ready, she'd answer his call when *she* was ready. Still, the pain inside her chest felt raw. Her jaw set, she disconnected the call.

She was still trying to catch her breath when she glanced in the mirror. The pale face staring at her made her gasp. She'd been here four days, and she still looked as if she spent her life cloistered inside Braxton College's hallowed halls. She grabbed a lipstick. A little color would make her look more like she belonged in Mardale.

From downstairs rose voices. One was deep, and she set her jaw against the emotion that washed through her. She definitely needed lipstick for this meeting, not that she was trying to impress Bryg Winslow, but she wanted to look presentable. She smoothed the pink color over her lips and dashed out of her room. At the top of the stairs, she felt someone watch her and turned to the room Zeke and Frankie shared. Zeke leaned against the doorjamb, his dark eyes filled with a pain he was too young to know.

"Do you need help with homework?" Leah asked the boy.

Zeke shook his head. His gaze shifted to the staircase before he stepped into his room and closed the door.

A quiver of alarm raced through Leah's chest. Did Zeke suspect a change was about to take place? After his unstable life, he didn't need another change. She'd talk to her parents about how to approach this concern. They'd make sure the boys knew the Rendell Ranch was their home until they graduated high school—Zeke and Frankie in a year and a half, Harry and Carl two years after that.

She took a calming breath and stepped to the staircase.

In the entrance stood Bryg, his powerful form filling the tiny area. He had a portfolio tucked beneath one arm. In his other hand, he held a paper bag. Leah's father took Bryg's coat, which had to be cashmere, and hung it in the coat closet. The jacket and pants he wore looked more expensive than the ones he'd worn this morning—the clothing Zeke had splashed.

Leah clenched her jaw, forced a smile, and moved down the stairs.

Bryg spoke to her parents, his manner easy and relaxed. When Leah reached the bottom step, Bryg lifted his gaze to hers and smiled.

Her heart picked up speed, and she chided herself that this man affected her. She'd met handsome billionaires before. She had to when the faculty hosted alumni fundraisers. *Those* billionaires never made her nervous. It was her job to convince the alumni to gift the college with generous donations, and she usually succeeded.

Tonight, the discussion would center on the town of Mardale, and Bryg's plan for this struggling community.

Bryg held up the bag to her. "I hope you don't mind, but I changed my mind about the clothes. If your offer still holds, and you think you can get the stains out, I'm willing to accept your offer."

"Yes, I'd be happy to do that." She took the bag, the guilt in her chest easing slightly. She set the bag on the table in the entryway. "I guarantee you, they'll look brand new."

"I'd settle for just the removal of the stains," he said, his mouth tipping in a way that made a strange sensation move through her.

Leah's father led Bryg to the living room and made small talk while Leah helped her mother serve tea.

"I appreciate your taking the time to meet with me." Bryg leaned forward in his chair and clasped his hands between his knees.

"We're always willing to hear what people have to say," Vern said, and Leah's head came up.

Looking at her parents, she noticed lines in their faces she'd never seen before. Her chest squeezed. After decades of working the ranch and taking in boys who needed help, they had to be tired.

"I appreciate that." Bryg pulled spreadsheets and professionally bound proposals from his portfolio. He handed copies to Leah's parents and her. "My staff ran some numbers, and this is the value they came up with for your ranch. I suggest you present this to your attorney for review."

Leah leafed through the proposal. Her eyes widened. She hadn't expected such a generous offer. Looking at her parents, she saw they were surprised, too. Bryg's features remained schooled, which she should've expected. A master negotiator, he would've learned long ago not to reveal any reaction during a business transaction.

"What do you think, honey?" Vern lifted his gaze to Leah.

"It's very substantial, which makes me wonder why." Leah looked at Bryg. This didn't look like an offer. It looked like a bribe, which would explain why Holly Johnson wanted to sell her ranch.

Bryg looked at Leah, but said nothing, which was an excellent tactic. It would give her the opportunity to talk, but this wasn't her ranch. Her parents would make the final decision. If they were ready to sell, she'd have to respect that.

"Since my parents own the ranch, and I don't, the final decision will be theirs, but I'm curious to know why you want to own land in a ranching community," Leah said.

"I'm glad you asked. Several companies are interested in building corporate centers in the area, because it's in the country, and it's near Denver. My team and I are still finalizing the plans, but we've designed residential communities and shopping centers that will complement the surrounding region. Once we've completed the plan, I'll release that information," Bryg said.

"You're aware other companies have presented similar plans to other towns only to abandon the projects." Leah studied his gaze, which showed no reaction. "That left the communities stuck with abandoned housing developments and shopping centers."

"That never should've happened," Bryg said, remorse in his tone. "And I'll make sure Mardale doesn't endure the same fate."

Leah's mouth flattened. The response sounded automatic, as if he'd said that to the other owners in the area. She looked at her parents. If they asked her opinion, she'd give it. Right now, she didn't want them to do anything until they knew Bryg's plan. She'd tell them that, too.

"Then, I guess we'll wait to hear what you want to do with the property," Vern said.

Something flickered in Bryg's eyes. Had Leah's father said something Bryg hadn't expected? She tried to hide the smile she felt. Her father had always been forthright.

"Maybe you'd like to see the rest of the ranch," Leah said.

"I've seen the area with the satellite pictures," Bryg said. He picked up his portfolio.

A wave of disappointment poured over Leah like cold water. Glancing at her parents, she saw in their faces what she felt—Bryg didn't plan to maintain the property as a ranch. Why look at anything when he planned to change everything?

"It's hard to see the inner workings from the satellite," Leah said and stood. "I'll give you a quick tour. It's still light enough, and the animals will be active. Taking care of them is work, but it never felt like that to me." She stepped to the coat closet and pulled out his coat and hers. "And I promise you won't get dirty."

She wouldn't take "no" for an answer and was surprised and relieved when he didn't argue.

"I trust you," he said, his laugh deep and sincere, and she wished it didn't make her like him more. He took her coat from her and held it open so she could slip into it.

Leah blinked. How long had it been since a man had helped her with her coat? Charlie had when they first dated, but that act of chivalry disappeared quickly. Was this Bryg's way to soften her, so she'd tell her parents to accept his offer? It wouldn't matter what she thought. Selling the ranch was her parents' decision.

"Thank you," she murmured.

"You're welcome." He smiled in a way that made her heart flip over.

She looked away. "We won't be gone long," she said to her parents and led Bryg through the kitchen and out the backdoor.

He stopped at the edge of the deck and looked around. His gaze swept over the yard that sloped gently to the barn.

Was Bryg visualizing the changes he'd make once he owned the place?

"It's beautiful, isn't it?" Leah looked at him. Beauty should take priority over profits.

"Yes, it is," he said, his gaze resting on her in a way that was decidedly unsettling, "but don't worry about what will happen to it. I'll preserve the essence of the ranch."

"I don't know that my parents will agree to sell their property to you. If they do, I hope you'll preserve this rugged beauty, though I think that will be hard with homes and businesses packed together." She looked at him and wondered at the intensity in his eyes.

"Let's see the animals," he said and extended his hand toward the barn.

She released a slow breath and moved down the path. She didn't know how, but she'd make Bryg understand the importance of preserving the gently rolling plains.

When they reached the barn, a loud snort sounded from the pen at the end of the barn.

"You have pigs?" Bryg's voice filled with surprise.

"You didn't see the pen in the satellite pictures?" Leah looked at him and smiled.

"Apparently not," he said and studied the pen. "And there's no smell."

"Because pigs are clean animals," Leah said. "Their health is important for proper breeding. That welcome you heard came from Miss Piggy."

"I like the name," Bryg said, and chuckled, a deep, soothing sound that made Leah's heart trip.

She wished she could hear that chuckle again and again.

"We've had a few Miss Piggies," Leah said. "I think this sow is our tenth. We've given different names to other sows, but this one is our favorite."

"I can understand why." Bryg looked at her, his blue gaze thoughtful and caring. "It's a name that evokes elegance and determination."

"These pigs can be determined." Leah laughed softly.

Miss Piggy lifted her head from the trough and looked at Leah and Bryg as if wondering what they were saying about her. Around her sounded the squeals of her piglets, their tiny heads bobbing around her. She nosed them out of the way, then dropped her snout to the trough.

"What about the piglets?" Bryg asked. "Do you have names for them?"

"Not unless they're good for breeding. Once they have names, we become attached to them," Leah said as she watched the piglets crawl over each other to get to their mother. Anxious squeals rose from the pen during the struggle. "If they don't have names, it's easier to send them to market."

17

"What do the boys think of the pigs?" Bryg asked with a raised brow.

"At first, they're not too crazy about them and especially cleaning up after them. Most have never owned animals. Not even a dog or cat, but once they learn how to care for the animals, they become attached. They're usually surprised to learn animals can have personalities like humans." She looked at Bryg and wondered what he knew about animals. Did he spend any time at his thoroughbred farm? If he did, he'd know the horses would each have their own personalities.

The skirmish in the pen grew louder, and Leah frowned.

"Don't tell me there's trouble in paradise." Bryg looked at her. The corner of his mouth tipped, though his eyes held concern.

"Someone isn't happy," Leah said. "I'll be right back." She stepped through the rails of the riding corral. She heard footsteps behind her and looked over her shoulder. "You should probably wait here. These animals can be unpredictable, and I don't want you to ruin another set of clothes."

"I'll be fine," he said, his smile confident.

The squeal grew louder, and Leah broke into a run.

A flash of pink squeezed from beneath the pen's slats and dashed across the corral. The piglet stopped in the middle of the enclosure and looked around. As if realizing it had found freedom from the crowded pen, it ran in a circle then toward the rails—toward the prairie bordering the ranch.

"Oh, no." Leah dashed after the piglet. "It can't go out there. It'll never survive."

"I'll get him." Bryg's arms and legs pumping, he ran passed Leah.

"But your clothes." Leah ran after him. She felt responsible for his first ruined set of clothes. She wouldn't let him ruin another set.

"I'll be fine," he shouted, and scooped up the piglet.

The tiny creature yelped and squirmed. A loud snort sounded from the pigpen. Miss Piggy nosed her brood aside and peered through the bars. She released a wailful howl. The other piglets stilled.

Bryg juggled the piglet that pawed at his coat as if determined to pursue its new found freedom.

Leah braked to a stop, her lungs heaving for air. She gasped at the mud stains the piglet left on Bryg's coat.

"Let it go." Leah tried to shout past her air starved lungs.

Bryg glanced at her, his eyes wide with surprise. The struggling piglet scrambled at Bryg's shoulder. Bryg twisted around. His legs slipped to the side. The piglet clutched to his chest, he turned in the air and thudded to the ground.

CHAPTER 3

*L*eah gasped at the motionless Bryg lying flat on the ground.

The piglet, briefly stunned, fell quiet, then struggled in Bryg's clutches.

"Are you all right?" Leah rushed to Bryg's side and dropped to her knees. Panting, she looked over Bryg's motionless form. She lifted the startled piglet from his grasp.

As if exhausted from the struggle, the piglet collapsed in her arms.

"I think so." Bryg's voice was thin and strained. His eyes closed. He lay so still, Leah trembled.

"Don't move. I'll be right back." Leah rested a hand on his, which was cool and tense.

Her chest tightened at the pain on Bryg's face. Jumping to her feet, she rushed to the pen and set the still stunned piglet next to Miss Piggy. The mournful sow sniffed her baby as if to confirm it had survived the adventure unscathed. Leah adjusted the pen's slats so the piglet wouldn't try another escape, which was almost guaranteed. She brushed dirt from her hands and looked down at her sweater. Miraculously, she'd avoided the mud and water that covered Bryg. She raced back to him and dropped to her knees.

"Did you break anything?" she whispered hoarsely.

Bryg opened his eyes and stared at the sky. His gaze shifted to hers. "I don't think so," he said, his voice rough. He didn't move. He breathed hard, and that made Leah's heart hammer.

"Maybe I should call an ambulance," she whispered.

"No," Bryg rasped. "I'm okay." He struggled to his elbows.

"Let me help you." Leah rose and extended her hand.

He looked at it as if doubtful she could help him stand.

"I can help." She looked at him and tipped her hand toward him.

His mouth curved before a grimace of pain spread over his face. Leah felt that pain to her core.

He rested his hand in hers, and the strength in his touch made her tighten her jaw. She leaned back, pulling on his hand. He rose to his feet.

"Your clothes," Leah murmured on a soft exhale. Her gaze swept over the pristine garments now stained with dirt and brown water. Mud covered his shoes.

Bryg's gaze followed hers. He gave a soft snort and lifted one foot. A stream of water poured out of the sole.

Leah lifted her gaze to his and pressed her lips together. "They're ruined."

"I suppose you know of a way to clean these, too?" he said with a lift of his brow.

"I do, though, I'm afraid these might be beyond salvation," she said softly. "The shoes definitely are."

"I think you're right," he said. He set his foot on the ground. A squishing sound followed. He gave a soft laugh and looked back at the pigpen. "How's the piglet? And please don't tell me he's scarred for life."

"He is a she, and I think Babe will be fine," she said with a laugh that held no humor.

"Babe?" His eyes widened with question. "You've given her a name?"

"I know I'm not supposed to," she said and pressed her lips together, "but she was so cute when she squeezed out of the pen and discovered she was free. Kind of like that old movie about the pig. Did you ever see that?"

"I believe so, and you're right. She was kind of cute, though I'd never thought I'd say that about a pig." He laughed, then winced.

A wave of emotion plunged through Leah. She didn't like that he was here to convince her parents to sell their ranch to him, but she didn't want him to hurt.

She took in a slow breath. "Let's go back to the house. I'm sure I can find some clothes for you to wear so you don't have to sit in those things."

"If you can loan me a towel, I can sit on that when I drive back to the house."

"You should at least change." Leah frowned at him. "Those clothes have to feel miserable."

"I'll be fine," he said. "I don't have that far to drive." He extended his hand indicating she should lead the way.

"I'll walk around the house to my SUV," Bryg said. "I don't want to track mud through the house."

Her parents and the boys were standing on the deck when they reached the house. When he told Leah's parents he was leaving, her mother offered to get his portfolio and slipped inside. She returned a moment later and handed it to him.

"What happened to you?" Zeke leaned against the backside of the house and tipped his chin toward Bryg.

"I lost a battle with piglet." Bryg smiled at the boy.

The boys broke into laughter and pushed each other, except for Zeke. His mouth curved slightly, as if he appreciated Bryg's humor and honesty. It was the first time since Zeke had arrived at the ranch that Leah had seen a light in his eyes.

"I'm going to get him a towel." Leah stepped toward the house.

"I'll get it, honey," her mother said and disappeared inside. She reappeared a moment later and handed Bryg the towel. "Are you sure you're all right?"

"Physically, yes. Unfortunately, I can't say the same thing for my pride." Bryg brushed the towel over his coat sleeves, then held it out to Leah.

"Keep it," Leah said with a laugh. "You'll need it more than we will." She glanced at the luxury SUV parked in front of the ranch house. "You may want to sit on it so you don't get your car dirty."

When she turned back to Bryg, she noticed the boys had moved beside him. With longing looks in their eyes, they craned their necks to view the vehicle's sleek lines, polished finish and gleaming wheels. Interest even sparked in Zeke's stony face.

"If you want to bring the clothes back, I can remove those stains," Leah said and tried to smile past the remorse hooked inside her chest. Because of her, two sets of his clothes were ruined, though she knew she could salvage the jacket and slacks he'd brought to her this afternoon.

Bryg gave a dismissive wave, then stopped. His smile pressed thumbprint dimples into his firm jaw. "All right. If you're sure it isn't too much trouble."

His smile broke her tension, and she released a soft breath. "It's the least I can do. I feel responsible that two sets of your clothes have been ruined."

She couldn't forget the fear in Zeke's face when he'd realized what he'd done, but what did she expect? He was a kid.

"They're just clothes." Bryg's soft voice edged through her thoughts.

"Maybe to you." Leah snorted softly. What those clothes had cost would cover ranch expenses for a couple of weeks. "If you want to bring them back tonight or tomorrow, I can work on the stains, but you should bring them soon. If the stains sit on the fabric too long, they'll be harder to remove, though I'm sure I can still get them out."

"Bring them back tonight," Leah's father said. "You can stay for dinner, if you don't mind a full table."

That brought Leah's head up. "Dinner?"

"Dinner?" Surprise sounded in Bryg's voice. He shifted his gaze to Leah as if asking her permission.

Around them, the restless boys elbowed and shouldered each other as they exerted their dominance.

Zeke stood away from the others, his bearing sullen, and leaned against the house. The other boys ignored him, though Leah knew they got Zeke's message—he'd confront anyone who challenged him. He was still testing the boundaries set up by Leah's parents, and she knew he'd soon test their rules.

Leah moved between Frankie and the other boys, her height and firmness stilling them with enough surprise to keep them quiet for a few minutes.

She felt Bryg's questioning gaze on her, and she lifted a shoulder. "Sure, come to dinner, if you don't mind meatloaf and mashed potatoes." She doubted that would thrill him. He probably had a personal chef who prepared organic entrees for him every night.

"That sound's great," he said and looked as if he appreciated the invitation. "I'll bring dessert."

The boys jerked their gazes to him.

"What will you bring?" Zeke's flat voice didn't hide the interest in his eyes.

Bryg shifted his questioning gaze to Leah and her parents. "What should I bring?"

"Tiramisu," Zeke said before anyone could answer. His mispronunciation didn't confuse what he wanted, though Leah wondered if he realized what the dessert was.

"Tiramisu?" Bryg said. If the request had surprised him, he hid it well. He arched a questioning brow at Leah.

"Actually, the bakery in town does sell it," she said, though she doubted it was on the list of Mardale-must-have desserts and wondered if that was the latest creation Danielle had learned during her last culinary class.

"Tee-a ..." Frankie stumbled over the word, then scowled. "What's that?"

Bryg pulled out his phone. A picture popped up on his screen, and he tipped it to the boys who crowded around.

Zeke glanced at Bryg's phone, then looked away. "Yeah, that's it."

"Is it any good?" Frankie asked.

"'Course, that's why I want it." Zeke shook his head.

When Frankie looked hurt, Leah draped an arm around his shoulder. "It is good."

She should know. She'd indulged in the dessert many times at a teashop near campus. When she had attended bridal bootcamp, she'd cut dessert from her diet. She'd been determined to fit into the beaded wedding dress that still hung in her closet in her Massachusetts condominium. Disappointment seeped into her chest. She didn't have to worry about fitting in that gown anymore, though since returning to Mardale she'd easily lost more weight than at any bridal bootcamp. And she didn't have to. What a waste!

"If that's agreeable ..." Bryg looked from Leah to her parents.

"Fine with me." Vern lifted a shoulder, and Leah wondered if he remembered what tiramisu was. She'd taken her parents to the teashop a couple of times when they'd visited.

"I like it. I think the boys will, too," Leah said. If they didn't, the freezer was packed with ice cream.

"Fine, I'll pick up the tiramisu on my way back here," Bryg said. "What time should I come?"

"Six o'clock should be fine," Vern said. "The boys will have finished their chores by then."

That made Zeke's eyes widen. He'd grumbled this morning when asked to clean the boys' bathroom that he'd only used once—not enough to make him clean it. When he learned television and computer privileges would be revoked, he'd cleaned the room. His grumbling was heard in every corner of the house, which wasn't unusual. Many boys before him had voiced their objections. Others would follow ... unless her parents sold the ranch.

When Zeke grumbled, the other boys ignored him, though Frankie had told him that if he'd do the work instead of complain, it would go faster. Zeke muttered something that made Frankie's face tighten. His jaw set, he shook his head, but walked away. Frankie had been at the Rendell Ranch long enough to know he should avoid a fight.

"I'll be back at six," Bryg said and lifted the towel. "Thank you for this. I'll bring it back."

"Keep the towel. Just remember to bring the clothes, so I can get the stains out." Leah gave him a slight smile. "They won't be as good as new, but they'll be close."

"Anything would be appreciated," Bryg said, his mouth curving faintly. "I'll see you at six." With towel and portfolio in hand, he climbed into his SUV.

"Come on, boys." Leah guided them toward the back door.

"Can we ride in Bryg's car?" Zeke didn't move. He stared after Bryg.

Leah looked back at Bryg. He was beautifully and wonderfully made, and her gaze lingered on him longer than she'd intended. Zeke noticed and gave her a hard stare.

The heat rising in Leah's face was so hot she knew she'd turned beet red. She had to remember these boys noticed everything. They'd lived on the streets. For them, paying attention meant survival.

"We'll ask my parents. If they agree, we can ask Bryg, but remember, he may not agree," Leah said.

The disappointment showing in Zeke's eyes caught the corner of Leah's heart. Disappointment was nothing new to these boys.

Sadly, she knew disappointment. It had slapped her in the face when she'd caught Charlie with his assistant. The shock had been devastating, but now made her realize that catching Charlie in the act had saved her from a terrible mistake.

BRYG SPREAD the towel over the driver's seat and climbed in. He looked back at the house and caught Leah looking at him. The halo of curls didn't conceal a face that easily spread into a warm smile. Her dark eyes held a tenderness he hadn't seen in a woman in a long time. Leah's kindness and caring attitude made her stunning.

One of the boys, Zeke as he remembered, hadn't missed Leah watching Bryg leave.

Bryg gave a soft laugh. Growing up, Bryg had been the same way. He didn't miss anything.

When he looked back at the house, he noticed Zeke said something to Leah that made her turn away. Bryg flattened his mouth. He wanted to look at Leah, but he'd see her at dinner tonight. That would make any meatloaf and mashed potato dinner taste like a feast, though he loved meatloaf and mashed potatoes. When he returned to his New York penthouse, he'd add those items to the menus his personal chef gave to his assistant each week.

He looked down at his clothes and wondered what miracle Leah could perform to get the stains out. Even if she couldn't clean them, it gave him the opportunity to discuss with Leah's parents a sales price for the ranch. If they weren't ready to sell, the right price might change their mind. His staff had provided background information on the ranch owners in the area—Vern and Mavis Rendell included. Now in their fifties, they'd owned the ranch for more than thirty-four years—four years before they'd adopted Leah's older brother, David. Two years later, they adopted Leah.

Even after spending an afternoon with the Rendells, he hadn't missed their devotion to the boys and to the ranch. A swallow slid down Bryg's throat. Leah and her brother were the lucky ones—the ones who were brought into a family who loved and cared for them.

The same love and care Bryg had received. If it hadn't been for Adam and Cheryl Moore, he wondered if he'd be alive today.

Something hot rose in Bryg's throat. The Moores had opened their home to him and had offered love and guidance. They had recognized his technical skill and had bought him a computer. By the time he entered college, he'd studied the stock market and as a college freshman had earned his first million.

Bryg might have been luckier if his real father, the man he couldn't remember, hadn't left. His mother had always told him his father was handsome and kind, but apparently not interested in sticking around. If his father had stayed, Bryg may not have made a few million before he graduated college. He swallowed hard. Having a father was the priceless gift he'd longed for.

That he had earned a few million as a college student had shocked him and opened his eyes to what some women in his college class wanted—a man with a few million.

After Bryg's mother left him, he believed money would help him get what *he* wanted—his parents. When he'd made enough money to find out what happened to them, it crushed him knowing his mother had been found dead in an alley. His father drifted around the country and even to Mexico a few times, but never settled down. He'd never been interested in finding out what had happened to his son.

Or maybe he knew and didn't care.

Bryg drove the SUV down the county road, thankful he'd only be in Mardale a few more days. This place brought back memories that should've been good. The foster family who had taken him in had helped him to understand the value of an education and had taken him to church, something he didn't have time for anymore. The bad memories were knowing he grew up without his parents.

Feelings of abandonment came rushing back at him. He'd get these sales deals wrapped up and head back to New York. Once the contracts were signed, he'd have no reason to return to Mardale. He'd hand the details over to his staff. He already had other prospects waiting to be negotiated—his favorite part about the deals he pursued. He loved dealing with the people, getting to know the area.

Best of all he loved returning to New York and throwing a party to celebrate his success. That the moneyed set clamored for an invitation to his parties amused him, and he wondered if any of his friends knew where he'd started. As long as he had money, they wouldn't care.

Maybe someday he wouldn't care either.

Driving past the fields filled with horses and cattle, a strange peace came over him. These people had little, yet everyone he'd met had a joy he envied.

Golden eyes and a lush smile wavered in his mind.

Leah Rendell.

Pure delight filled her face. He saw that look in his foster parents' faces, and the people he met when they'd taken him to church. Normally he spent Christmas with them, their children and grandchildren, but this year they volunteered for a mission trip. A great emptiness rose inside him, and he wondered how he'd spend the holidays. His assistants would send the Moores a card and a donation so they could buy something extra for their grandkids. They'd always handwritten their thanks and invited Bryg for a visit.

Being around the Rendells and their foster children reminded him of how fortunate he had been. The Moores had given him so much. His hands tightened around the steering wheel. He wouldn't let business interfere with his relationships with people he cared for. As soon as he wrapped up the contracts in Mardale, he'd visit Adam and Cheryl before they left for their missions trip.

When Bryg reached the house he'd rented, he showered and changed and collected the ruined clothes. He'd wash the towel and return it the next time he visited them—he hoped there'd be a next time.

In town, he stopped at the florist and picked up a bouquet of red roses, then went to the bakery where the baker packed the tiramisu in a pastry box.

Bryg was surprised at the rise in his chest when he parked in front of the Rendell's home. It felt more like a date than a business meeting.

The boys must have seen him coming because they piled out the front door. Even Zeke stepped to the porch, his hands in his pockets. Leah rushed after the boys, her dark hair springing around her anxious face, and making Bryg's heart rise in his chest. She warned the boys to be careful of Bryg's clothes. That made the boys cautious, but didn't dampen their curiosity. They jumped around each other, trying to glimpse the SUV's interior.

Bryg climbed out. He left the door open so the boys could look inside. Later, if Mavis and Vern agreed, he'd take the boys for a drive.

He walked to the backend. The boys rushed after him. When the hatch floated open, Bryg pulled out a canvas bag.

"What's in there?" Frankie frowned as if wondering if he should be excited.

"My dirty clothes," Bryg said and laughed when Frankie made a face. He held out the bag to the boy. "Would you be kind enough to carry these into the house for Leah?"

"Sure," Frankie said in surprise and took the bag.

Bryg pulled out the bouquet and pastry box. All the boys quieted and stared at Bryg. Even Zeke, who kept his distance from the group, watched Bryg's every move.

"Roses!" Frankie's eyes stretched wide.

Bryg didn't miss Leah's surprised look.

"They're beautiful," she murmured and lifted her gaze to his.

Beautiful like Leah, Bryg thought. The softness in her eyes filled Bryg with an emotion he'd never felt before and wanted to feel again. And it made Bryg wonder when was the last time Leah had received roses. Too long, but he'd fix that. He'd text his assistant to schedule a delivery before he left Mardale.

"It's very nice of you to bring all this." Leah slipped the pastry box from his hand.

The boys jostled each other to peer through the box's plastic window. The surprise in their faces showed they weren't quite sure what to make of the fluffy swirls of cream and the chocolate shavings. Their surprised glances turned into I've-seen-tiramisu-before expressions.

"Since your parents invited me to dinner, and you offered to clean my clothes, it's the least I can do," Bryg said. He liked the light in her eyes. If the boys weren't staring at him, he'd never stop looking into that dazzling gaze.

"Don't thank me for cleaning the clothes yet," Leah said with a laugh. "But I did work on the stain on the clothes you wore this morning, and they look pretty good, so I'm sure I can get these stains out."

The smile curving her lips was the most beautiful thing Bryg had seen in a long time, and the surge of feelings flooding him made him take a steadying breath.

"Let's go inside." Leah guided the curious boys away from the SUV and extended her hand toward the front door.

Zeke waited until the other boys had gone inside before he pushed away from the wall and sauntered after them. Mavis and Vern stood in the entry way.

Mavis' face filled with surprise when she saw the roses. Her appreciative gaze lifted to Bryg. "They're lovely. I'll put these on the table so we can enjoy them during dinner."

"Have a seat." Leah gestured toward the living room. "I'll put the tiramisu in the refrigerator. Would you like something to drink? I made raspberry tea."

"Raspberry tea sounds wonderful," Bryg said, and followed Vern and Mavis into the living room.

"Come on, boys." Leah tipped her head toward the kitchen. "You can help me serve the tea and put dinner on the table."

The boys pushed into the kitchen except Zeke, who remained in the entryway, his eyes narrowed, his posture defensive. Bryg gave him a slight smile. He recognized the reluctance in the boy's eyes. When he first went to live with the Moores, he had challenged them.

"Everyone pitches in with dinner." Leah smiled at Zeke. She extended her hand to the kitchen indicating she'd follow him.

When Zeke glanced into the living room, surprise flickered in his eyes to see Bryg, Mavis and Vern looking at him. He shouldered away from the wall and sauntered into the kitchen. There was no condemnation and no relief on Leah's face when she followed him.

Bryg tucked in the corner of his mouth. Leah seemed to be used to the challenge the foster kids raised—a far cry from most of the students at her private college where their biggest concern would be earning grades that would open doors to careers at prestigious firms. Bryg should know. Every day, he received those students' resumes and accompanying letters describing what they had to offer his company.

He sat in the living room and made small talk with Vern and Mavis, but didn't miss Leah's graceful movements as she and the boys stepped in and out of the kitchen. Even though she wore casual pants and a sweater, she moved around the table with elegance and dignity. There was something about her that seemed to calm the boys as well.

After the meatloaf dinner and tiramisu dessert that seemed to taste nothing like the boys had expected, including Zeke, whose surprise showed in his wide eyes, Bryg helped clean the kitchen.

Leah's mouth dropped open when he offered, though she said nothing. He had a feeling she rarely kept her opinions to herself, but apparently thought showing gratitude would be a better example to set before the boys.

With the kitchen cleaned and the boys settled in their rooms to complete homework and get ready for bed, Bryg sat in the living room with Vern, Mavis and Leah.

"I, that is my parents and I." Leah nodded to her parents but still looked at Bryg. "Would like to know what you'll do when you own all this land. That's assuming anyone in the valley agrees to sell their ranch to you." Her calm voice didn't hide the caution in her eyes.

"Nothing's firm yet." Bryg relaxed into a winged chair. "But I'll work with you and your parents and the other landowners to make sure the proposal benefits the valley. The population here is aging and not many young people stay in the area." He wouldn't add that she had moved away. Judging by the look in her eyes, she was aware she was one of the young people who chose not to live in Mardale, but for some reason she was back here now. She had said she was on Christmas break from the college, but the pain in her eyes made him think there was another reason.

"Have you visited any of the ranches you want to buy?" Leah asked.

"Not yet," he said slowly. "This is the first, though I have communicated with some other owners." He'd spoken with Holly Johnson, whose ranch bordered the Rendell's. Public records offered the information he needed about the other ranches in the area. The Rendell ranch was the largest, and the Rendells had the respect of the community, making it a good place to start so other owners would feel more receptive when he approached them.

"Maybe it's time you got to know the ranches a little better." Leah stood.

"What did you have in mind?" Bryg said cautiously. He stood, too.

"We should finish the tour we started this afternoon," Leah said. Her smile warmed the inside of Bryg's chest.

For a moment, he wondered what it would be like to see that smile every day. That took him by surprise. Never had he met a woman whom he wanted to be in his life every day.

"But don't worry. We won't be chasing piglets." Ah, her musical laugh. "I'll take you to the barn and you can meet the horses. The boys like taking care of them best. They learn to ride and care for them, which takes their focus off themselves and onto something else."

"I'd like to see the horses," Bryg said, and he wouldn't mind a private moment with her—only because it gave him the opportunity to explain he wanted nothing but good for the community.

"We won't be gone long." Leah glanced at her parents.

"Take your time. It's been a long day. We'll check on the boys and call it a night. It'll give us more time to consider your offer." Vern looked at Bryg.

"I'd be happy to answer any questions you may have." Bryg didn't want lingering doubts to prevent them from selling. They weren't a young couple. Taking care of the ranch and taking care of foster children would exhaust anyone. Though Leah's parents showed commitment to these boys, Bryg's offer would give them the retirement they deserved.

"We don't have any," Vern said, "but we can talk more in the next day or so. Stop by anytime."

Bryg watched them leave. He would talk to them soon. Locals had told him the Rendells were the anchor in this town. Though Vern was the town mayor, he and Mavis looked out for others while running the ranch and raising foster kids.

Just like the Moores.

Bryg helped Leah put on her coat and then slipped into his own. The outside air was cool, and he liked breathing in the freshness that he missed since moving to New York. When he was in the city, he rarely went outside. His driver took him to his office or the club where he met friends for a game of squash.

When he visited his home in the Hamptons, he spent time outdoors, but not without his phone and not without conducting a business deal.

He and Leah walked through the crisp air and down a path to the barn. The inside almost looked like a home with its clean aisles and stalls. The smell of fresh hay hung in the air. Horses nickered and poked their velvety noses through the Dutch door openings.

"This is nice," Bryg said and noticed Leah hadn't missed the surprise in his voice.

"It has to be to give the boys a clean environment to live and work." Leah smiled at him.

She hadn't told him anything he didn't know. He remembered social services coming to inspect the Moores' home, yard and other things he no longer remembered.

Leah stepped to a barrel filled with apples. She scooped a few in her hands and offered him one. "You can't visit horses without giving them a treat."

"You're right," he said. When she placed an apple into his open palm, the tenderness in her touch pierced him.

She didn't seem to notice. Instead, she smiled at him and stepped to a stall.

"This is Ginger," Leah said and stroked the horse's mane.

The horse whinnied and tipped her head as if wanting more of Leah's gentle touch.

Bryg's mouth curved. He'd known Leah less than a day, but being near her filled him with a warmth he wanted to hold close.

Leah opened the stall door and stepped inside. Bryg followed. Except for his thoroughbred farm in Kentucky, he hadn't been around horses much. Lately, he hadn't had time to spend on his horse farm, but there would be time for that when he retired. If he retired. The thrill of closing a deal brought more satisfaction than sitting around and staring out the window of his New York penthouse, his beach home in the Hamptons, or his vacation villa on the Côte d'Azur.

And if he lived in this quiet community in Colorado? That made him catch his breath. He was here to make a deal and revitalize a vanishing community. He'd close the deal and board his jet to New York, where he belonged. Something uncomfortable scraped the inside of his chest, and he wondered at the connection he felt for a place he'd soon leave and wouldn't think about in the next week or two.

"How're you doing, girl?" Leah opened her palm beneath the horse's mouth. The mare delicately worked the apple between her teeth, then nodded as if showing gratitude. Leah dug her fingers into the soft hair between the horse's ears and the horse closed her eyes.

Bryg understood that. Even without feeling Leah's touch, he knew there was meaning at the tips of those delicate fingers.

The horse gave a rough snort and turned away, her hip striking Leah.

Leah gasped. Her arms flung wide, and she tipped backward. Bryg held out his arms. He caught Leah and held her close. The warmth and softness that pressed against his chest literally took away his breath.

CHAPTER 4

*B*ryg sucked in air, Leah's subtle scent sending a shock wave through his chest. Her soft curves made him tighten his jaw.

When the horse shifted her large frame, Bryg pulled Leah firmly against him and stepped toward the door. Her warmth filled him, and he didn't want to let her go. Ever.

"I'm sorry," Leah murmured. She twisted in his arms and pressed her hands to his chest.

Bryg thought she'd push away, but when she lifted her gaze to his, she stilled. Bryg drank in the large eyes filled with a softness he'd never seen when he'd looked at any woman.

"Are you all right?" Bryg asked, his voice rough. *He* wasn't all right. His gaze dropped to full lips he had an overwhelming desire to taste.

"Yes," she said slowly.

An anxious whinny sounded from the neighboring stall.

"The horses." Leah's voice breathless, her eyes wide, she pressed her hands to his chest.

Reluctantly, Bryg loosened his grasp and let her step away. His jaw set at the coolness that swept away her comforting closeness.

"It sounds like they're keeping tabs on each other," Bryg said with a laugh.

"They're like kids," Leah said and smiled. As if the moment of their closeness had been forgotten, she brushed fingers through the silky hair that had fallen over her cheeks. "They know who's getting special treatment and aren't shy about expressing their dismay."

Maybe she'd forgotten the moment he held her. It would be awhile before he did.

"Let's feed the others," Leah said. Turning away, she stepped out of the stall.

A muscle worked in Bryg's jaw, and he tried to pretend his arms didn't ache to hold her. They moved down the stalls and fed apples to the other horses. When they reached the end of the aisle, Leah looked out the large picture window that faced a small building surrounded by a slatted fence.

"I'm assuming that's the chicken coop." Bryg stood next to her.

"Yes, there's nothing better than farm fresh eggs," she said and released a soft sigh. "Fortunately, the college where I work is in a town that sells fresh eggs at the co-op, but they never tasted quite as good as the ones we raised."

Bryg wondered at the distant look in her eyes. Did she miss her home back east, or was she glad to be back on this Colorado ranch? He was glad she was here, otherwise he might not have met her, but he still wondered at the pain in her eyes. He wished he could erase the moment that had filled her with sadness. She was so beautiful when she smiled. If she were the woman in his life, he'd want to see her smile every moment.

"Why did you leave the ranch?" he asked, though he had read her profile on the college website. Born and raised in Colorado, she'd attended the exclusive college. While she studied for her master's, she also taught. She became a professor while working on her doctorate.

"I was offered a scholarship to Braxton College," she said, a distant look in her eyes, "which was a surprise. I couldn't have attended a private school without it. When I applied to the master's program, they offered me a teaching position. After I received my doctorate, I stayed. I love the town, the students and the college. I thought I'd stay forever." Color flooded her face, the telltale sign she'd said more than she intended. She looked away. "Maybe it's a good thing I came back..

"Why is that?" Bryg said. In her eyes, he could see the distant memories reminding her of what she liked about the ranching community. "I'd forgotten how much I love it here." When she smiled, there was a hint of sadness. "I guess you can take the ranch girl out of Colorado, but you can't take Colorado out of the ranch girl."

"I wouldn't want Colorado taken out of you," he said. When her head came up, he smiled.

"What about you?" she asked, and he saw her determination to switch the conversation away from herself. "I know you're from Denver, and that you started a successful business when you were in college."

"Ah, you've done your homework," he said on a soft exhale. Apparently, he wasn't the only one who wanted to know about the people he dealt with.

"Not that I had to do much. After all, you are Bryg Winslow," she said her mouth tipping with a hint of guilt. "It's difficult to be on the internet for any length of time and not see at least one article about you."

His mouth flattened. That had been *his* disappointment. He hadn't worked hard so he could become media fodder. At a young age, he learned he didn't have to be poor, and he'd do anything to make sure he and those he cared about would never want for anything. Being young, single and rich caught the media's attention.

It wasn't just his business dealings that fascinated the press. It was his personal life. When he saw photos of himself holding the hand of some supermodel, movie star or socialite, his stomach clenched. Though the media loved to publish stories about his business and his personal life, they got nothing right.

"I'm sorry." Leah's eyes widened with an embarrassed apology. "I didn't mean ..." Her voice faltered as if afraid the more she said, the more uncomfortable she became.

"You've no reason to apologize." Bryg smiled at her, hoping to ease her discomfort.

No one had been more surprised than he when he'd first seen his picture headline a media site, a beautiful movie star clinging to his arm. He hadn't expected the famous actress to say yes when he'd asked her out. His disappointment was a weight in his chest when he soon learned these women weren't dating Bryg Winslow, the poor kid wishing he had a bike and wearing clothes his mother had dug out of a rummage sack. He was Bryg Winslow who turned every business venture into a pot of gold. With the endless parade of people who pressed around him wanting whatever he had, his financial ability seemed more like a curse than a blessing.

"Something tells me your notoriety isn't that appealing to you." Leah lifted eyes filled with sympathy to his.

"Is it that obvious?" he said with a dry laugh. He dragged his fingers through his hair.

"Yes," she said on a heavy exhale.

"I'd like to think that if I'd realized how my life would've changed, success might not have been that appealing to me, but then hindsight is always twenty-twenty," he said simply.

She looked at him a long moment, then her gaze shifted.

"I get the feeling you have something to say about that," he said and tipped his face to look into her eyes. He loved the depth of them and the compassion in them, and suddenly he knew when he left Mardale, what he'd remember more than anything else were the golden eyes and the pale skin covered with freckles of one Leah Rendell.

"I do, but about something else, too," she said, and the corner of her mouth curved. "The day after tomorrow is Sunday."

"Yes," he said, and wondered at the reason for her mentioning this.

"We attend church on Sundays," she said, her eyes large, and he was struck by how fresh and innocent this college professor looked right now. "You're welcome to join us if you'd like."

Church?

How long since he'd been to church? The Moores took him and the other foster children to services every Sunday. At first, he'd refused to attend, which didn't matter to the Moores. He was going. That he liked it, surprised him, but he liked everything about church, including the people and the message. He'd gone a few times in college, but then became distracted by his studies. Now, he only went when he visited the Moores.

He lifted a hand to dismiss the invitation. He didn't just have this project in Mardale to settle. He oversaw other ventures. Tomorrow, he'd fly to Boise to check the progress of a development there. Even if he didn't have to leave, he received reports throughout the day that needed his review and approval. Since he'd started his first business when he was in college, Sunday had been the day when he analyzed his financial progress—a ritual he'd maintained over the last fifteen years.

"I appreciate the invitation …" He looked into her eyes and saw the understanding. He was saying what he'd heard many times when he'd invited people to church. He gave a soft laugh, and then to his surprise, he said, "Thank you. Let me know where and when, and I'll meet you there."

CHAPTER 5

*S*unday morning, Leah and her parents escorted the four boys to the youth group in the church basement. She wondered if Bryg would come. She hadn't heard from him in two days, though she'd heard plenty about him. Whenever his private jet flew in and out of the community airport, local tongues wagged. She never commented. She wasn't interested in what he did, though she listened to every word when it came to Bryg Winslow.

Frankie, who had dressed carefully in his new-to-him clothes, made an entrance that caught everyone's attention, including the cute blonde he always sat next to. He rushed to her and spun around, then spread his arms wide as if ready to accept her admiration. She laughed shyly, the color rising in her cheeks making Frankie stare at her as if she were the most beautiful woman he'd ever seen.

The other boys dashed across the room to join friends, except Zeke. He stood in the doorway. Surprise, then obstinacy, covered his face. He'd still be in bed if Leah hadn't explained he wouldn't just miss church, he'd lose privileges. That got his attention. Now the stubbornness returned.

"Where are you going?" Zeke's mouth set, and he lifted his dark gaze to Leah.

"To the church service in the sanctuary," Leah said. "Come on, I'll introduce you to Pastor Chuck." She tipped her hand to a broad-shouldered man standing at the front of the room and talking to several of the kids.

"Pastor?" Zeke's surprise gave way to a slight smirk.

A deep voice sounded from the end of the hall, Bryg's voice, and Leah sucked in a soft breath. She hadn't realized she'd made a sound until Zeke's face came up. He looked past her, surprise rising in his face. He cast Leah a questioning look. She smiled and hoped she looked as if Bryg's coming to church was the most natural thing in the world. She'd invited and believed him when he said he'd come, but his being here still caught her off guard.

Several feminine voices blended with Bryg's, and Leah realized he'd caught the attention of several women. She couldn't blame them. His perfect features looked as if they'd been chiseled by a master sculptor. Everything about him radiated profound and stunning masculinity.

Bryg smiled and chatted with the women, but looked over their heads and nodded at her as if confirming he'd join her soon.

Leah's palms went damp, and she took a deep breath. She was glad Bryg had accepted her invitation, so why was she suddenly nervous? Even when she'd presented her dissertation before an unsmiling faculty, she hadn't felt this uneasy. Her throat suddenly dry, she swallowed. Bryg was a friend—sort of—not a faculty member who could make a decision that would impact her career.

She felt an intense stare. Glancing to the side, she saw Zeke's narrowed gaze studying her.

"Ready to go meet Pastor Chuck?" she asked. She forced a smile ——a feeble attempt to rein in her emotions. She wouldn't let Zeke or anyone else know how Bryg's presence affected her.

"I'm not going in." Zeke's jaw jutted.

"Do you want me to stay in here with you?" Leah understood Zeke's reluctance. He'd come from a tough Denver neighborhood and had probably never met anyone like these farm and ranch kids. He wasn't the first boy who'd resisted going to church. He wouldn't be the last.

"I'm not a baby." Zeke's eyes narrowed coldly.

"No, you're not," she said on a soft exhale, her heart aching for the pain she saw in Zeke's face. "Let's go upstairs. We can sit in the sanctuary."

"I'm going home." Zeke kept his voice low, but his dark look attracted glances from the surrounding kids.

And from Bryg. Leah saw him excuse himself from the group of women. His stride purposeful, he crossed the room to Leah and Zeke. He greeted Leah, then extended his hand to the teen. "Zeke, how's it going?" He spoke gently, his eyes warm and with an interest that showed Zeke was important to him.

Zeke's head came up. He blinked in surprise, and his anger seeped away. "Okay." He looked around as if confirming Bryg spoke to him. Slowly, he slipped his hand into Bryg's and shook it.

A lump rose in Leah's throat. This billionaire wasn't just charming. He had a heart.

"What are you doing here?" Zeke gave Bryg a suspicious look.

"Probably the same as you." Bryg looked straight into Zeke's large and vulnerable, brown eyes, his smile kind and compassionate. "I was invited."

When Zeke looked at Leah, she lifted a shoulder. "I did invite him."

Bryg looked past the teen to the kids milling about the open area. Most stood in groups and talked. Some helped Pastor Chuck set up the props he'd use for his let's-get-acquainted mixer, something he did for the Rendell foster kids since the local kids knew each other. He also used props for his sermon.

"Should we find a place to sit?" Bryg arched a brow at Zeke.

"I guess." Zeke looked over his shoulder. He watched the kids for a moment.

The uncertainty in the teen's eyes made Leah press her lips together. He'd been taken out of his surroundings and introduced to a group of kids who wouldn't know what his life had been like, and he knew nothing about theirs. Glancing at Bryg, she saw he hadn't missed the doubt clouding Zeke's face.

"Will you join us?" Bryg smiled at Leah.

"I'd love to." Leah couldn't hold back the joy she felt at seeing Zeke warm up to Bryg. Too bad he wouldn't stay. Hopefully, by the time he left, Zeke would accept he was in Mardale to stay, at least for a while. "I'll tell my parents that I'm staying down here so they don't wonder where I am, but I'll be right back."

Leah raced up the steps greeting friends and neighbors as she strode to the sanctuary, but in the back of her mind pounded the question, who was Bryg Winslow? How many times had she seen photos of the billionaire flashing a confident smile for the cameras? Never had she seen him without a stunning woman on his arm.

A twinge of shame squeezed her chest, and the flush rising in her cheeks made her want to fan her face. She was judging him. She'd only known Bryg the man for two days. Bryg the billionaire she thought she knew, but his interaction with Zeke shattered her preconceived notions. She had assumed the almighty dollar ruled his life. She hadn't expected him to accept her invitation to attend church, but here he was and sitting in a youth group with dozens of hyperactive teens.

After telling her parents she and Bryg would attend the youth service, she rushed downstairs. In the lower room, she saw Bryg standing in the center, a group of teens surrounding him. Zeke stood next to him, a pleased look on his face.

When Pastor Chuck asked everyone to take a seat, Bryg asked Zeke where he wanted to sit. Zeke seemed surprised that his opinion mattered, but led the way to where the other foster kids sat.

The pastor opened with prayer, then engaged the youth group in a whirl of games and conversations that brought laughter and amusement. Leah watched Zeke, and her heart lifted when he seemed to enjoy himself.

It wasn't until after the service that Leah found herself standing next to Bryg. She noticed he watched the boys chat with friends, and she couldn't help smiling when she saw Zeke had found someone he wanted to talk to. Had Zeke turned a corner? Would he accept the ranch as his new home? Her heart buoyed inside her chest. She hoped that wasn't too much to ask.

Several volunteers set up tables and set platters of cookies and punch bowls on top. Families from the sanctuary and the children's ministry crowded into the room.

"You're thinking about him, aren't you?" Bryg's voice was quiet.

When Leah lifted her gaze to his, the concern in his eyes scooped air from her lungs. A faint smile curved his mouth.

"I think about all the boys, but yes, I'm thinking about him." With reluctance, she looked back at the boys. "They've endured a lot in their short lives. I'm so proud of my parents for devoting their lives to these lost boys, but ..."

"But you're concerned about the toll it's taking on your parents," Bryg said, compassion in his tone.

"Yes, I'm glad I have this opportunity to help them, but next quarter I'll return to Braxton," she said softly, then looked at Bryg. "I'm glad you came today, not just because of Zeke."

"I'm glad I came, too," he said, a distant look in his eyes as he looked over the families laughing and talking. "It's been awhile ... a long while."

She watched him, not just because he was handsome, so handsome she found it difficult to breathe, but because of the way his intelligent eyes took in the relaxed atmosphere—probably a far cry from his high-powered board meetings.

As if he felt her gaze, he looked at her, his expression bemused, questioning.

"Sorry." She felt the heat rise into her cheeks. She was twenty-eight years old, had a doctorate and still blushed. "I didn't mean to stare." She just couldn't help herself.

"I like that about you." His mouth twitched.

"That I stared at you?" She gave a nervous laugh. How could she have been so rude?

"Well, that." He spoke with such tenderness. "I'm glad there's something you find worth looking at, but a woman who blushes is quite refreshing."

Leah wanted to fall through the floor. How many times had she blushed in Bryg's presence? A lot, but she hadn't thought he'd noticed.

He noticed. He didn't miss anything. He hadn't missed Zeke's agitation.

"I thought I would've outgrown that by now, but *I* am doomed to blush." She shook her head and offered a smile that felt dry.

"I find it charming," Bryg said, and his mouth curved.

She gave a soft snort and looked away. At least *he* did.

"What will you do this afternoon?" she asked. She wanted to get the attention off herself.

"I have some papers to review." The response sounded automatic, and she wondered if he'd been reviewing papers for so long he hadn't even thought about what he said. Did he enjoy reviewing these papers, or was this a way to keep from thinking about something else?

"If you want to take a break from all those papers, stop by the house," Leah said. "We have a late Sunday lunch." The invitation was out before she could stop herself. The caution in her inner voice made her wish she'd kept quiet. The wound Charlie had marked on her heart was still fresh and raw, yet she couldn't deny her attraction to Bryg, which was just that—an attraction. He was nice and engaging, and interested in buying land for a business deal that would add to his wealth.

She couldn't retract the invitation. Her family always had an open door for neighbors and strangers and boys trying to find their place in this world.

Bryg's eyes flickered, and she thought he'd decline the invitation. She held her breath.

"I'd like that." The gentleness in his voice was almost her undoing. "What time should I come?"

"We eat around three, but come whenever you want." She inhaled deeply to quell the shaking in her stomach.

"All right," he said, "I have a few calls to make, and then I'll come by. What can I bring?"

"Just yourself. Mom and I usually prepare more than we can eat. With four boys in the house, we have to be prepared, so come hungry." She uttered a soft laugh. She was feeling nervous again. She lectured to packed auditoriums. Hundreds of students enrolled in her classes. How could she feel nervous talking to one man?

A silly question. She knew why. When she was near Bryg, the thin grasp she had on the emotions rising inside her snapped.

"Then I look forward to having lunch with you and everyone else," Bryg said. He gave her a smile that made her want to sigh.

"Where are you going?" Zeke stood between Leah and Bryg, his hard stare zeroed in on Bryg.

Leah had noticed him standing with Frankie and talking to a group of kids she'd seen around town. Actually, Frankie talked. Zeke stood next to him, his gaze moving over the other people in the room. Leah hadn't seen him say anything, but he'd seemed more engaged than she'd seen him since he'd arrived in Mardale.

"Back to the house I rented." Bryg said. When Zeke frowned, Bryg said, "It's where I'm staying while I'm here, but I'll see you at lunch. "

Zeke blinked, then relaxed into his that's-cool stance.

Bryg extended his hand to the teen. "You'll be there?"

Zeke shifted his gaze to Leah, then shrugged. "I guess."

Frankie and the other boys raced over to Bryg and crowded around him, all asking questions at once. Bryg's face glowed, and he patiently answered their questions—his smile easy, his eyes filled with interest.

Leah's chest filled with a heartfelt intensity. She was relieved that Bryg had earned the boys' trust. When they raced off to talk to other kids, Bryg told Leah he'd see her at lunch, but Leah had a sense he didn't want to leave. That made this feeling rising inside her even more concerning. She didn't want to feel anything toward Bryg or any man.

She watched Bryg walk up the stairs, his stride purposeful and decisive. He greeted several people as he left.

Leah needed to take a breath. When she turned away, she saw Zeke watching her, his gaze narrowed.

Her heart kicked up a notch. She smiled at him. "Ready to go home?"

Zeke said nothing but stared at her. What did the boy see? Something she didn't want to admit to herself?

"Sure," he said, and turned and walked toward the other boys.

Leah released a slow breath. She'd get her emotions under control. She'd done it when she'd set her engagement ring on top of the bookcase in Charlie's office.

She'd fallen in love once, and for that her heart had been broken.

Her jaw set.

Never would she let her heart become vulnerable again.

CHAPTER 6

*L*eah scoured her mother's pantry for items that would remove the stains from Bryg's clothes. She mixed a solution and applied it to the spots. After blotting them a few times, the fabric glowed like new. The guilt in her chest lifted as she inspected the clothing then placed the jacket and pants on hangers. The garments looked almost as good as they had when Bryg wore them. She hoped he agreed.

Her phone rang, and she glanced at the screen. She took a breath when Charlie's name pulsed in the frame. The ache in her chest throbbed with each sound.

Was she ready to talk to him? No. He had betrayed her. Would she ever be ready to talk to him? She hoped so. She couldn't avoid the inevitable. They both needed to move on with their lives. She had thought he had, but then why was he still calling?

She wouldn't build her future on what her life might have been if she and Charlie had married. She reached for the phone. It stopped ringing. Slowly, air seeped from her lungs.

Her ex-fiancé had called several times and always left messages of profuse apology. The inside of her chest felt raw and scraped. Maybe he *was* sorry. She had to call him back, though she wasn't sure what she'd say. That she forgave him? She didn't feel like forgiving him.

She murmured a prayer that the words would come when she did call Charlie, then swallowed against the memory emblazoned in her mind. What surprised her was that she wasn't sure she *was* sorry she'd caught him with his assistant. Because of his indiscretion, she'd had a chance to think of what she really wanted to do with her life. Marrying Charlie didn't rise to the top of that list.

She had looked forward to the wedding and to starting a family, but spending the rest of her life with Charlie? Somehow she'd never thought of the marriage in that way. Even if Charlie hadn't betrayed her, she shouldn't have placed her focus on the children they'd have. When she and Charlie *did* speak, she'd explain to him that maybe her catching him with his assistant had saved them both from a terrible mistake.

After covering Bryg's clothes with a dry cleaner bag, Leah went to the kitchen to help her mother. Her father and the boys were in the barn completing the afternoon chores. On the counter sat a covered bowl filled with rising dough. She punched it down then shaped small pieces into dinner rolls. She covered the tray with a cloth and set it on the counter so the rolls could rise again.

As she worked, she thought of Bryg and how much he had enjoyed working with the children in the youth group that morning. *That* had been a surprise. He was polished and sophisticated and didn't seem like someone who would enjoy the games or listening to Pastor Chuck's sermon. The teens loved being near him. Even Zeke had stood nearby.

After he left the church, Leah chatted with Holly Johnson, who seemed anxious about something. As they talked, Leah realized the sale of her ranch caused her concern. She shared with Leah the price Bryg had offered, which gave Leah a start——it was almost as generous as the one he'd offered her parents.

Leah's heart felt like a cold stone weighing inside her chest. Bryg wouldn't make these offers if he didn't expect to make a sizable profit.

But selling the ranch wasn't Leah's concern. The ranch belonged to her parents.

For years they had operated the ranch and raised foster children. They never complained. Raising the children and working the ranch brought them joy, though Leah struggled with the toll the hard work had taken on her parents. They were in their fifties and didn't move as quickly as they used to. After their years of dedication, they should think about retirement. Bryg's timing couldn't have been better. His offer would make her parents' later years very comfortable.

Leah lifted the slow cooker's lid and inhaled the pleasant odor of roast beef, potatoes, carrots and onion. The aroma washed over her in a wave of loss. She missed her mother's cooking. She loved to cook, too, but with her teaching schedule, it had been easier to order a meal on her phone app or spend an evening with Charlie and friends in a restaurant than cook an hour or two in the kitchen.

"He's here," Frankie shouted from the barn.

Leah's head came up, and she set the slow cooker lid down hard. Her heart drumming in her chest, she smoothed clammy hands over her slacks and glanced around the kitchen.

"Everything will be fine." Her mother's smile always had a way of putting her at ease.

"Thanks, Mom." Leah offered her mother an apologetic smile and basked in the compassion shining in her mother's eyes. "Everything's always fine when you're in charge."

"You know how to cook a good meal." Her mother pulled a stack of dishes from the cabinet. "That apple pie you baked makes my mouth water."

"As much as I'd like to take credit, you did most of the work." Leah reached for the plates her mother held.

"I'll set the table." Her mother smiled and tipped her head toward the door. "You greet our guest."

Leah glanced out the window. Bryg climbed out of the SUV, a bouquet of roses and baby's breath in his hand.

The boys shouted and raced out of the barn to welcome Bryg.

Except Zeke. He sauntered but watched the other boys who talked at once and leaped around Bryg.

Bryg's laugh made Leah watch him a moment longer than she'd intended. She gave her head a slight shake. With everyone he met, he seemed glad to know them, to spend time with them, even with these boys who came from nothing. Everyone at the church liked him. It didn't seem to matter the real reason he had come to Mardale.

Despite the boys' excitement at seeing Bryg, Leah felt rattled. Everyone in town had bemoaned the residential and commercial centers that had replaced the serene farms and ranches in the neighboring towns. Those communities were closer to Denver, so Mardale residents had thought no one would be interested in changing their picturesque town.

But townsfolk hadn't realized that when they sent their children away to college, those children would prefer the excitement of the city to small town tranquility.

Just like Leah. Her mouth dried, and she tried to swallow the disappointment rising in her throat.

When she'd received the college scholarship, she'd planned to return to Mardale and teach. Instead, she'd stayed, earned graduate degrees, and joined the faculty. After this Christmas break, she'd return to the college.

Leah grabbed her coat from the closet and stepped to the front porch. Her father walked up the path from the barn and shook Bryg's hand, then indicated they should walk to the house. When Bryg turned, his gaze met Leah's. His smile turned brilliant. Her heart soared.

Trying to still the pounding in her chest, she gave a slight wave ——the country way of greeting people. Now that she was home, her college sophistication slipped away. You can't take Colorado out of the girl.

"Hey, boys, give Bryg some breathing room," Leah said with a laugh.

The boys froze, looking from her to Bryg.

"They're fine," Bryg said. He climbed the steps to the deck and handed her the flowers.

"You're spoiling us," she said, and inhaled the sweet fragrance that mixed with the crisp air. "They're beautiful. Thank you," she murmured, and didn't miss the boys clasping their hands and fluttering their eyelashes as they mimicked her.

"Your day's coming," Bryg said to the boys and laughed.

Leah laughed, too, then turned to the house.

"Can you take us for a ride in your car?" Zeke asked Bryg.

"Well ..." Bryg glanced at Leah's father.

"Okay with me." Vern tipped his head. "We'll eat supper in about half an hour.

He hadn't finished speaking before the boys dashed to the SUV.

"Do you want to go?" Bryg looked at Leah.

That shocked her. That she wanted to go shocked her more. "Sure." She lifted her shoulders.

Her father slipped the bouquet from her hands and said he'd take them inside.

"Let Leah sit in the front," Bryg called after the boys who turned to him.

The surprise in their eyes vanished, and they jostled each other while clamoring into the SUV.

"Don't worry, guys. There's a window seat for everyone," Bryg said. He walked Leah to the passenger side and opened the door for her.

She didn't know if she should be suspicious or pleased. Buttering her up would be a good way to get her parents to agree to sell the ranch to him. She released a soft exhale. She wouldn't let Charlie make her doubt another man's kindness.

"Thank you," she murmured and climbed into the car.

"My pleasure," he said simply, the softness in his eyes drawing heat into her face.

They were taking a quick drive. She wouldn't make it more than that.

The boys suddenly quiet, she looked over her shoulder at them.

Awe filled their eyes as they ran their hands over the plush upholstery and pressed the levers that adjusted their seats.

"Is this your car?" Zeke asked when Bryg climbed behind the steering wheel.

"Zeke, you shouldn't ask that," Leah said softly.

"It's all right." Bryg grinned and looked into the rearview mirror. "It's a rental car, but I'll use it while I'm here in Mardale."

"I'll have a car like this someday." Frankie lifted his chin. Determination shone in his eyes.

"Me, too." Harry and Carl chimed in.

Zeke said nothing. He stared out the window——at the snow covered meadows, but Leah didn't miss the determination and drive that burned in him, and she wondered what secret plans he was making.

He still kept to himself, but the suspicion in his face wasn't as intense as it had been the first day he'd arrived. It hurt Leah that he still felt the need to be cautious. She hoped one day he'd learn to trust. She also hoped all the boys would learn that real treasure was in heaven, but that realization took time. Her parents worked patiently with each boy that came to them to make sure they understood God's grace.

"Where's a good place to go?" Bryg asked Leah when he guided the car to the country road.

"The bluffs are close. It's cold and windy there now, but the views are spectacular."

"Then that's where we'll go," he said, and sped down the road.

After a few turns, Bryg parked on a snowy flattop that overlooked the prairie stretching to the mountains. Denver's skyline rose in the distance.

"Can we get out?" Frankie asked, his hand on the door handle.

"For a few minutes," Bryg said, "but we have to make it quick, since supper is almost ready."

The boys piled out. Even Zeke seemed excited. Their breath white clouds rising into the cold air, they scooped up snow and flung snowballs at each other. Their shouts and laughs mixed with the dull thuds when the snowballs hit their marks.

Leah stood and stared at the white prairie stretching before them. Never had she thought about the day when she wouldn't see it anymore.

"You love this place." Bryg's deep voice broke through her thoughts.

"I do." She turned to him. Her breath caught when she saw the concern in his eyes. She looked away. Wasn't she being like the boys? Giving more importance to physical things than to what really mattered?

Vaguely, she was aware of the boys' shouting and racing about. She started to turn to them when Frankie shouted, "Look out."

Her head came up. An icy ball zeroed straight toward her. She ducked and turned. Her toe hitting a snow-covered rock, she tipped forward and gasped.

Strength and warmth wrapped around her waist, lifted her and pulled her to a muscled wall. Bryg held her close, the arch of his body shielding her from the snowball and the cold. A soft thud sounded against his back and echoed inside her head. His powerful form had taken the brunt of the snowball and spared her.

Shock rolled through her. Had a man ever sacrificed himself for her sake? A slight tremble rocked through her chest. Never.

"Are you all right?" Bryg tipped her back and stared into her face.

"Yes." She couldn't stop staring into intense blue eyes.

The rising silence made her feel as if they were the only ones here, but they weren't alone. The boys were here. She glanced sideways to see four pairs of eyes staring at them. She cleared her throat.

Bryg looked up. The intensity in his eyes turned to humor. His deep laugh sent a surge of emotions through Leah that she fought to push down. Her pulse rocketing, she stepped from him, breaking the grasp that had filled her with comfort. She gave a nervous laugh and fingered damp hair from her face.

"You saved her," Zeke murmured, his dark eyes darting from Bryg to Leah.

The other boys stared at Leah and Bryg, their gazes intent.

Leah froze, her throat hot and tight. Zeke had said what she couldn't admit to herself. Bryg had stepped between her and the snowball.

"I did what any man would do, but Leah's a strong woman. She can take care of herself," Bryg said. He clapped his gloved hands together, sending fragments of snow into the air. "Let's get back to the ranch so we can eat."

The boys laughed and shouted and scrambled through the snow. They piled into the SUV, the snowball fight, and Bryg's chivalry, forgotten.

Bryg extended his hand, indicating he'd follow Leah to the SUV. She gave him a hesitant smile and trudged through the snow. When she looked up, she saw Zeke staring through the window at her, then Bryg, and she saw in his eyes that he would remember what Bryg had done for her.

She gave Zeke a slight smile, but inside she still felt Bryg's warmth and his comforting strength, and she couldn't help but wonder what lucky woman would feel that for the rest of her life.

CHAPTER 7

At the house, Leah led the boys and Bryg inside to an aroma of roast beef and freshly baked bread. Her parents' voices sounded from the kitchen.

The boys shrugged out of their coats, hats and gloves, and headed for the dining room.

"Upstairs, first," Leah called after them. "Wash your hands and comb your hair." Feet pounded up their stairs, followed by running water with an occasional demand to use the sink and the mirror.

Bryg helped Leah stow the outerwear into the closet.

"It smells wonderful in here, and it's making me hungry," Bryg said, his smile casual and tender. The thumbprint dimples pressing into his cheeks made Leah's heart tip over.

"Good." Leah turned away so he couldn't see the color rising into her cheeks. She led him into the dining room her mother had set so immaculately it almost looked like the five-star restaurants where she and Charlie had dined.

The boys gathered around the table while Leah and her parents set the carved roast beef, a tureen filled with steaming vegetables, a bread basket and a salad in the center.

The relaxed and casual meal followed the blessing with Bryg as interested in what the boys said as he was in talking to Leah and her parents. After dessert, Leah's mother asked the boys to clear the table. When Bryg helped, the boys stared at him open-mouthed.

"You may need to tell me where to put things," Bryg said to them and winked.

Their eyes bright, they were more than happy to tell him what to do. When they finished, Leah started the dishwasher and told them to work on their homework. They groaned. They wanted to spend more time with Bryg. Leah couldn't blame them. Bryg was interested in everything they said and did. With reluctance, they followed Leah up the stairs. She made sure they understood their homework before she returned downstairs.

In the living room, her parents spoke to Bryg in low tones, and Leah slowed her pace. They were discussing the sale of the ranch.

"The attorney is looking over the offer," her father told Bryg. "We can let you know our decision in a couple of days."

"That's all I ask," Bryg said and rose. He thanked them for the meal.

"Let me get your clothes. I checked them several times and think I removed all the stains," Leah said, and dashed up the stairs.

When she returned, she held out the hangers holding the clothes.

Bryg's eyes widened with surprise. He lifted the hangers from her hands, the strength in his fingers radiating through her, and she took a quick breath to still the jump in her pulse.

"I don't know how you did it," he said, his look direct, "but thank you."

"You shouldn't thank me." She shook her head. "I feel responsible."

"Don't," he said gently. "They look great. I appreciate what you did."

"You're welcome." She couldn't help but smile at the appreciation in his eyes. "I'll walk you out." She took her coat and his from the cloak closet and led him outside.

"Why do I get the feeling you have something to say?" Bryg asked her when they walked down the front steps to his SUV.

Leah gave him a quick look, but his comment shouldn't have surprised her. He was a man completely aware of his surroundings.

"Holly Johnson told me about your offer to buy her ranch," she said and looked into eyes that seemed to offer an apology.

"I did. I don't know that you can put a price on a lifetime of work, but I think what I offered her was fair," he said, his tone sincere. He hung the clothes in the back of the SUV. When he turned to her, his gaze was direct.

"Maybe, but is it comparable to what you'll make when you develop the land?" She studied him. She hadn't meant to be so direct, but was relieved Bryg's gaze remained steady and even.

"In my business, everything's a risk." He took her hand and gave it a tender squeeze.

She didn't pull away. His touch was gentle yet firm and filled her with a warmth that scooped air from her lungs. Charlie's touch never felt like this.

He released her hand, and she set her jaw against the cool air that swept away his touch.

"You seem to know when you should take the risk and when you shouldn't," she said.

"Not always, but I have been doing this for a while, so maybe I've learned a few things along the way," he said and looked straight at her. "If you like, I'll email you my plans for the entire area. Nothing's been finalized. Since your father is the town mayor, he'll give final approval before we approach the other ranchers. Everything's been designed to fit in with the terrain."

"I'm sure you saw the plans the developers submitted to the other communities," she said, knowing he would have. Someone like Bryg studied everything before beginning a project.

"Yes." He looked at her as if knowing what she'd say next. "And I saw what happened to those communities."

"So you know those communities lost their country charm," she said, and wished she could keep the heartbreak out of her voice.

"Trust me," he said, and the sincerity in his eyes almost made her believe she could. "I won't let that happen."

She released her breath softly. By the time the development began, he'd be in another part of the country, or world, and would've delegated the project management to someone in his office.

"I'll oversee everything to make sure it goes according to plan," he said as if reading her mind.

She blinked. Never had she met a man so intuitive. With business, Bryg would have to be. He couldn't have built the Winslow empire without being aware of what others were thinking and feeling. So why couldn't she calm the unease rising in her chest?

"I keep my word, Leah," he said raggedly. Slowly, so slowly, he intertwined his fingers with hers.

The touch filled her with a longing she hadn't felt before, and she didn't want it to ever leave. She didn't pull away, but she didn't curl her fingers around his. She let the feeling soak through her skin and pulled it deep inside her. The warning bells she wanted to ignore sounded faintly in the corner of her mind. She'd trusted Charlie. She thought they'd marry Christmas Eve. Instead, she was back at home and with a man she could fall hard for if she didn't keep the walls around her heart in place.

As if sensing her inner turmoil, Bryg slowly released her hand. "My staff will submit a final plan to me in a couple of days. Why don't we review it together? You can come to the house I'm renting. It has a large dining room where we can view the drawings, or I can come here."

"When will you start the project?" she asked.

"If everything goes as planned, next summer," he said. The twinkle in his eyes relayed the excitement he felt about this venture.

She gave a soft exhalation. That meant all the ranches would be replaced by glass storefronts and homes with three and four car garages. Should she care? She wouldn't be here. She was teaching a summer class at Braxton. After a brief break, she'd start her fall classes. Her parents wouldn't sell the ranch until all the boys had graduated and were on their own. After that, she wouldn't spend Christmas in Mardale. By then her parents would've bought their condominium in Florida, and Leah would spend the holiday strolling a beach …

… and remembering Christmases past when she'd bundled up to work in the barn, go to church, and take sleigh rides with her friends.

Already, she missed Mardale.

"I have an idea," Bryg said, and she looked into eyes that truly seemed to care. "How about I give you a seat on the board? That way, if you have an objection—"

A loud shout from an upstairs window cracked the ranch's serenity. Leah gasped and turned to the house. Shadows of flailing arms and entangled forms passed behind the glass. More shouts sounded.

Leah broke into a run, but heard Bryg's pounding footsteps behind her. She jerked open the door. Her parents were crossing the living room when she dashed across the entryway and bounded up the stairs two at a time.

In the hallway, Harry and Carl peered through the door leading into the bedroom Zeke and Frankie shared. Their eyes wide, they jerked their gazes to Leah and stepped back. Leah burst into the room. Zeke straddled Frankie on the floor, his fist raised.

"Zeke, no!" Leah had wanted to shout, but could barely catch a breath to speak.

A strong arm, Bryg's arm, reached past Leah. He wrapped a hand around Zeke's upper arm and pulled him to his feet. He led the boy to the other side of the room and released him, but his powerful form remained a barrier between the two boys, as if leery the fight wasn't over.

Leah noticed her parents usher Harry and Carl to their room, though they stared through the doorway as long as they could before disappearing.

"What happened?" The calm in Leah's voice barely concealed the thrashing inside her chest.

"He keeps throwing his stuff on my bed. I told him to keep his junk on his own side of the room." Frankie breathed hard. He shook his hair into place and straightened his rumpled shirt.

Leah arched a brow at Zeke, who rolled his eyes and looked away.

"You need to show respect for Frankie's belongings. If you need more room, talk to Vern or Mavis or me." Leah looked into dark brown eyes. Her heart ached knowing the stony expression concealed pain she couldn't imagine, but that she'd seen in other boys her parents had raised.

Vaguely, she was aware of Bryg moving into the hallway.

"I'll talk to them." Leah's father walked into the room.

Leah nodded. She stepped into the hallway and closed the door. She didn't see Bryg. From the next bedroom, she heard her mother's soothing voice talking to the other boys. Soon her father's reasonable voice sounded from behind the closed door, followed by Frankie's anxious tone. If Zeke said anything, Leah didn't hear him, but the boy's silence spoke volumes.

She moved to the top of the stairs and saw Bryg standing in the entrance.

"Sorry about that." She walked down the stairs, but still listened to her parents' quiet voices. She'd always been proud of the work they'd done with the boys, many of whom had gone to college and embarked on notable careers. A lump rose in her throat. Her parents couldn't do this forever. Who would do this after they sold the ranch and moved to Florida?

No one.

And what would become of the boys who needed this special care? That there were other places that worked with displaced youth provided Leah with vague comfort.

"No apology needed." The understanding in Bryg's eyes slightly eased the tension in Leah's chest. "Boys tend to test their boundaries." His hand on the front door handle, he looked at her.

Her mouth flattened, and she nodded. Frankie and Zeke weren't the first boys to scuffle. She released a slow breath. They may be the last.

"If you want me to stay …" Bryg looked at her.

"Thanks, but we'll be fine," she said. "We've worked through these problems before, and we'll probably …" Her voice trailed.

She and her parents wouldn't work through these problems again. She'd return to Massachusetts. Her parents would retire to Florida. What was this emotion rising inside her? Regret? Fear? She'd made her career choice. She'd always admired what her parents did. If it hadn't been for them, she and her brother would have ended up some place else. How blessed she'd been to be raised by Vern and Mavis Rendell.

She felt Bryg's gaze on her. The look in his eyes told her he knew what she was thinking.

"I'll walk you to your car. Again," she said, eager not to dwell on the hollow feeling opening inside her.

"No need," he said gently. "I'll call you as soon as I review the plans, and we can set up a time to get together. We can do it at my place or here."

"We should do it here," she said. "My parents should know what you plan."

"I agree. I have your parents' number. I'll call when everything's finalized." He gave her one last look and stepped out the door.

She stood in the entryway and listened to the steady hum of his SUV's engine as it rolled away. She turned from the door. Her parents walk down the stairs.

"Everything okay?" she asked them.

"Yes, boys like to see what they can get away with," her father said, but his eyes narrowed slightly. "Are you okay?"

"I'm fine." She gave a surprised laugh. She wasn't fine. She liked being home, but after the holidays she'd return to campus. She always had this struggle whenever she visited, but before she knew she'd spend her next break at the ranch.

How had a man she barely knew changed her world—and in more ways than one? She'd get rid of that thought. She wouldn't lose her heart to the man who was about to transform her life forever.

CHAPTER 8

*B*ryg drove down the country road. He didn't like that each turn of the SUV's wheels took him farther from the Rendell Ranch and farther from the woman who occupied his thoughts more than any woman he'd met.

Her golden eyes wavered in his mind. The hesitation in her voice echoed in his ears. His mouth flattened. What would it take to gain her trust?

She loved the ranch, and he understood why. It was a simple life she could return to whenever she needed to escape the city.

It intrigued him to see this college professor relax into the girl she would've been when she grew up on the ranch. He knew little about her except what he'd seen on the college website. After graduating from Braxton, she'd studied for her master's and worked as a teaching assistant. Some pictures of her at the college's fundraisers showed her standing next to a man Bryg learned was a prominent lawyer in the town.

The twinge rising inside Bryg gave him a start. He barely knew Leah, but knowing there was a man in her life made him wonder if that man appreciated this intelligent and gentle woman. Bryg had noticed a tan line around the ring finger of her left hand. He hadn't read anywhere that she'd been married. Engaged? If so, why not wear her engagement ring?

Because she was no longer engaged?

Something tugged inside his chest. He wanted to be by her side, ward off anything or anyone who might hurt her. Her strength was one of the many things that drew him to her, but matters of the heart sometimes slipped through the barrier. Those pains worked their way through unguarded openings, sliced deep wounds, then disappeared, though the scars showed in moments when reminders brought memories to the surface.

The eyes always revealed more than anyone realized. Bryg spent his life studying people, getting to know them, so he probably saw more than most.

He'd seen more in Leah's eyes than he was sure she'd intended. Looking at her had been pure pleasure, though his chest tightened when he saw those flickers of something that told a story she seemed to want to keep to herself.

His jaw set. He was here to complete a business deal, and one he'd make sure would follow the plan he'd discussed with Leah and her parents——the residential and commercial development would preserve Mardale's country charm.

He had promised Leah. He'd do everything he could to keep his promise, which was why he was still in Mardale. He'd planned to delegate the development to his staff. They were competent enough, but he wasn't ready to let go—because of Leah Rendell. He wasn't ready to leave Mardale, and he wasn't ready to spend even one day without seeing her. That day would come soon enough. If he were smart, he'd start preparing for that day now.

BRYG SPENT the next two days telecommuting with his staff to make sure the final plan was exactly what he'd promised Leah and her parents. When he'd finalized the plans, a weight lifted off his chest. He couldn't wait to share the drawings with Leah. He dialed the number to the Rendell Ranch.

"Hello? Bryg?" The distraction in Leah's voice made his chest tighten.

"Yes." Breath rushed from his lungs, and he stood. "Is everything all right?"

"Yes, I mean no. I mean, Zeke's gone," she said, and not with that calm, professorial tone he'd noticed the first time she'd rushed to him apologizing for the muddy water Zeke had splashed on his suit.

"When did he leave?" He strode across the entry and pulled his coat from the closet.

"This morning." She hesitated, as if trying to control the fear that edged into her voice. "We're so worried. He has a warm coat and gloves, but it's freezing outside."

"I'll be right there." He clutched the phone between his shoulder and ear and pulled on his jacket.

"Oh, no," she stammered. "I didn't mean to drag you into this. We've already called the sheriff. They're looking for him. I'm going to look for him—"

"Wait until I get there," he said, and dashed into the garage. After making sure Leah wouldn't leave until he arrived, he drove down the country roads but kept close to the speed limit.

When he drove up the Rendell Ranch driveway, Leah ran out the front door. No one else was around. Bryg climbed out of the SUV and strode to the porch.

"Is anyone else here?" he asked. He hated seeing the ashen color of her face.

"No, my mother took the other boys to town for a homeschool activity. My dad is out looking for Zeke." Tight lines pressed into the corners of her eyes. "The boys know Zeke's gone."

"I didn't see him walking along the road when I drove here," Bryg said.

"I don't think he's staying near the main road," Leah said. "When I checked his computer, I noticed he'd saved satellite maps of paths through fields and back roads. All the maps led to Denver to an area called The Grid. That's where he grew up."

Bryg's breath froze in his lungs. He was all too familiar with The Grid. It had been rough when social services took him from the walkup apartment he'd shared with his mother more than twenty years ago. He didn't want to imagine what it was like now.

"If he walks all the way there, he'll freeze to death." The quiver in Leah's voice made Bryg's chest tighten.

"I doubt he'll walk all the way," Bryg said.

"You mean, he'll hitchhike there?" Her eyes widened with alarm, making him wish he hadn't said anything.

Bryg took her hand, small and warm in his, and together they prayed for Zeke's safety.

"We called the police department there." She sounded a little calmer. "But they won't consider him missing until he's been gone forty-eight hours and even then, he won't be a priority. Runaways never are."

"Then we'll make sure we find him," Bryg said and didn't miss the quick look she gave him. He was glad he sounded calmer than he felt. He opened the SUV door for Leah and helped her climb inside.

He rounded the hood, his chest tightening with each step. Zeke may be a street smart kid, but he couldn't anticipate every situation he'd encounter. In that neighborhood, there were plenty of people who kept an eye out for a kid in need. Zeke wouldn't be a match for those predators.

"Engrave him in the palm of your hand, Lord," Bryg murmured. He climbed into the SUV and drove toward the country road.

"When did you notice he was missing?" he asked Leah.

"When the boys came back from working in the barn this morning." She stared out the windshield. "He went down there with them, but when they finished, they couldn't find him. They said they hadn't noticed him leave, and I think they're telling the truth. He's always been an outsider and kept his distance. The other boys still try to include him in conversations and games, but he likes being by himself, so they let him."

Bryg's mouth tightened. He remembered a few kids like Zeke at school and in the neighborhood. Growing up in a rough part of town taught him to be aware of his surroundings. Zeke would be like that.

"Do you have a picture of Zeke?" Bryg asked her.

"Yes, on my phone." She almost looked relieved. "I took it the day we went shopping in town … the day Zeke stepped into that puddle and splattered your clothes with mud." Her mouth tipped with regret.

"Don't worry about that. The important thing now is that we find Zeke." Bryg tapped an address into the car's navigational system.

"You know where you're going?" Leah looked at him in surprise.

"I know a few areas in Denver." And not ones he wanted to discuss. What did the neighborhood look like now? He swallowed hard. He was about to find out.

"I guess I shouldn't be surprised. I did look you up on the internet," Leah said. Her eyes were large, and there was a tinge of guilt in her voice.

"You don't need to apologize." He glanced at her and hoped his smile made her relax. "Everyone's on the internet these days. It's easy to find information about someone."

"Did you look me up?" There was a lift in her voice, and he felt her stare.

"I was curious," he said and glanced at her again.

He liked the intensity in her eyes. She wasn't afraid to confront anyone, a good characteristic for someone who taught college. Some students could be challenging. *He* had been.

"You graduated from Braxton top in your class," he said. He remembered everything he'd read about her. He found her interesting after their first meeting and wanted to know more about her. "The college accepted you into the master's program, and while you worked on your master's, the college offered you a teaching assistantship. They hired you full time when you worked on your doctorate. You've studied abroad, you taught at Cambridge, then you returned to Braxton. You've published several award-winning articles and two books that are required reading at a few universities."

"You *have* done your homework." There was a roughness in her voice, and her eyes went wide. Had she never become accustomed to life under the microscope?

"As I do with anyone I work with," he said.

She opened her mouth, and he knew she'd say he hadn't known he'd work with her.

"I know. Your parents own the ranch, not you, but before you and your brother graduated high school, your work with the foster children your parents have raised was commended. Your town paper always announced when you and your brother plan to spend the holidays in Mardale, so naturally, I assumed you'd be involved in any decision your parents made regarding the ranch."

He spent the next half hour guiding the conversation from her life on the ranch to her shock at receiving a scholarship to a private college to teaching at an overseas university. When they drove past the airport, the traffic closed in around them, but Bryg drove the SUV in and out of the slowing cars and never reduced his pace. They neared Denver's downtown skyline, and he exited to a boulevard that narrowed into a neighborhood filled with brick houses and storefronts that had to be a hundred years old.

He heard Leah's stomach growl and saw her place a hand to her middle, though she stared out the windshield.

"There's a diner up the street, nothing fancy, but we can grab a sandwich there." He looked at her.

Her full lips parted and color rose in her cheeks. The emotions rising in his chest made him catch his breath. If he weren't driving, if they didn't need to find Zeke, he'd cup her face and kiss her.

"I'd rather look for Zeke." She looked out the side window. "I just hope we can find him. There're so many places a kid can hide or …" Her face whitened.

His heart went rigid. Kids always thought they were invincible. He'd always thought that.

"We'll find him," Bryg said, and prayed again. He didn't want Zeke to spend one night in this place. When he looked at Leah, he saw the question in her eyes, and his mouth set. "We will." He couldn't promise, but he'd do everything in his power to do what he said.

He drove the car down a narrow street crowded with tiny houses. Jig's Corner Store, a place where Bryg used to hang out, stood next to the sidewalk. Bryg wondered if Jig still ran the store, or if he were still alive. He'd be old if he were. The store's display windows and glass door were covered with wrought iron bars. Next to it stood a building with plywood covering the windows. He felt Leah stiffen and wished he hadn't brought her here. She grew up in Mardale and now lived in a college town, a far cry from this rough place.

The streets were almost empty. Few people walked along the sidewalk. Fewer cars drove down the street. Bryg found a parking place in front of Jig's and squeezed into the tight space.

"Can you pull up that picture of Zeke on your phone?" he asked. "I'll see if anyone in there remembers seeing him."

"I'll go with you," she said, her hand on the door.

"It's better if you wait here." He looked straight at her.

"Zeke is my responsibility. I need to know what's going on," she said, her gaze intense.

"You will know everything. It would be easier for me to get information if I go in there alone." When she opened her mouth to object, he said, "Trust me. I know these people."

That seemed to catch her off-guard, and for a moment she kept very still.

"All right," she said, and lifted her chin. "But if you're not back in five minutes, I'm coming in."

His chest squeezed at the determination in her eyes. "I'll be back in five minutes." When she looked at him hard, he said, "I promise."

He expected an argument, but slowly her hand slid from the handle.

She pulled her phone from her purse and tapped the screen. "What's your phone number? I'll text you this picture."

He gave it to her, and she typed it in. A moment later, the notification sounded on his phone. He looked at the picture, at the boy who didn't smile and whose eyes were filled with the pain Bryg had seen many times during his years in the Grid.

"Thanks," he murmured and stepped out of the car.

Inside the store, Bryg gave a start when he saw Jig sitting on a stool behind the counter. His hair was almost completely gray and more lines edged into his face, but other than that, the store owner looked the same.

Refrigerated cases lined the walls of the store that was smaller than most bedrooms. The shelves behind Jig were filled with liquor and cigarette cartons.

"I know you," the old man said, his keen eyes widening.

"Hey, Jig, it's been awhile. How've you been?" Bryg extended his hand.

"Not bad. Bryg, isn't it?"

"That's right," Bryg said. Had Jig seen him on the news?

"What can I get you?" The man shook his hand and started to stand, but Bryg waved him back to his seat.

"I'll just grab some sodas and chips." Bryg picked out the items and set them on the counter. Jig watched him when he pulled out his wallet and then his phone. He tipped the phone's screen, still showing Zeke's picture, toward Jig. "Have you seen this kid?"

"Yes." Jig lifted his gaze to Bryg. "What's he done?"

"Nothing. I'm here to take him home."

"Are you a cop?"

"No," Bryg laughed softly. Apparently, Jig *hadn't* seen him on the news. "I just want to make sure he's all right. He has a nice home out on the plains. I want to make sure he gets back there safe and sound."

"You just missed him," Jig said, and rang up Bryg's purchases. He slipped the sodas and snacks into a bag and set it on the counter. "He came in. I asked him if I could help him, but he didn't answer. And he didn't buy anything. He just walked out of the store and headed toward Park Avenue."

Zeke didn't buy anything, because he didn't have any money. Bryg's throat closed. The poor kid had to be starving.

"Did he say where he was going?" Bryg asked, though he knew the answer. Zeke didn't say anything.

"Didn't tell me a thing." Jig lifted his eyebrows.

"Thanks," Bryg said, and threw a few bills on the counter. He picked up the bag and turned away.

"What about your change?" Jig called after him.

"Keep it." Bryg looked over his shoulder at the man.

"Thanks." Jig smiled. "And remember your friends. You know we'll always be here."

Bryg tipped the corner of his mouth at him. Maybe Jig remembered him after all. He rushed out of the store and climbed into the SUV.

"Jig saw Zeke." Bryg tried to sound calm, but knew he'd failed when he felt Leah stiffen.

"When?" Leah's voice was strained. She took the bag from him and set it on her lap. "Where?"

"Just a few minutes ago." Bryg started the SUV and pulled away from the curb. "He went into Jig's store but didn't buy anything."

"Poor kid," Leah said weakly.

"When we find him, we'll give him the sodas and chips I just bought. You can help yourself," Bryg said. He hoped his smile would reassure her. He gave her hand a quick squeeze.

"Thank you for doing that. I'm not hungry, but Zeke has to be starving," Leah said on an exhaled breath. Her slim fingers tightened around the sack.

Bryg released a slow breath. Hungry and other things. He had to make sure he and Leah found Zeke before someone else did.

He cruised down one street, then turned onto another. When he'd see people walking down the street, he'd stop the SUV and jump out, show them Zeke's picture and ask if they'd seen him. Some had. Some hadn't.

Bryg's frustration mounted. Where could Zeke have gone? The sun moved across the sky, which heightened Bryg's concern. He didn't want Zeke spending the night in this neighborhood.

The tension he felt from Leah gripped his own chest. He'd promised her they'd find Zeke, but where would the kid go?

And then he knew. The rec center. Kids in the area always went there. He'd often hung out there when his mother hadn't paid the rent, and the landlord locked him out of the apartment.

"I know where to find him," Bryg said. He hoped he was right. He didn't want to disappoint Leah, but he had to take a chance. His life had always been about taking chances.

"Where?" Leah asked. Hesitant hope filled her voice.

"A place where the kids always liked to hang out." Bryg guided the SUV around a corner.

Ahead, a lone form wearing slacks and a black jacket sauntered down the sidewalk.

"I think we made this too hard." Bryg slowed the car. Leah looked at him, then her gaze followed his. He heard her soft gasp and knew she'd recognized the clothes.

Bryg spotted a parking space along the street and squeezed the SUV next to the curb.

Leah reached for the door handle.

"Let me talk to him," Bryg said, his voice low and firm.

"I'm responsible for him," Leah said, and Bryg saw the heat of an argument rising in her face while she struggled to stay calm. "I accepted that you would talk to Jig alone, because you knew him. I know Zeke."

"You're right. You do," he said and looked into her eyes. "When I told you I'd looked up your background on the internet, you never said if you'd looked up information about me." He stared straight at her.

Her gaze dropped, and he had his answer. "Then you know I spent the first twelve years of my life in The Grid."

Even someone who grew up on an eastern Colorado ranch would have an idea of what life in The Grid had been like. She taught English literature and would've studied the famous works that revealed the desperate lives of the underclass.

Every starry eyed reporter that had interviewed Bryg always asked about his life in The Grid as if there were something romantic about growing up in the worst Denver neighborhood. The only good thing about his life in The Grid was that it had placed him in the Moores' foster home.

"Can you just give me a couple of minutes with him?" Bryg asked her.

He saw the swallow slide down the slender column of her throat and understood her struggle. She blamed herself for Zeke leaving, but she didn't realize Zeke needed something familiar. Now that he had it, he may have realized it wasn't as he remembered.

Leah's mouth worked. She pressed her full lips into a flat line and nodded. Bryg wrapped his hand around hers, felt the warmth and softness of her skin, and wished he could do so much more.

He climbed out of the car, looked up and down the street. Hands in his pockets, he followed Zeke, but felt Leah's concerned stare as if she touched him. He just wanted her trust, though he had a feeling even if he won her trust with his handling of Zeke, he'd have to work harder to earn her trust in an area that was becoming surprisingly important to him. Would he succeed? He looked after Zeke. First things first.

Zeke's pace was slow, and he kept his head down. Had he tried to find his friends but couldn't? Even a loner like Zeke would have one friend.

Bryg was a few feet behind Zeke, when the teen glanced over his shoulder. Shock, then mistrust, wavered in the teen's eyes, and Bryg expected him to burst into a run. Bryg looked closer. Zeke's eyes were red. The threat of hot tears shone in the kid's dark eyes.

"Hey," Bryg said, his throat filling with the emotion he saw in Zeke's face.

The corner of Zeke's mouth twitched, but he said nothing. He watched Bryg.

"Let's go back to the ranch." Bryg tipped his head as if the ranch were just down the street.

Zeke didn't move. He looked past Bryg to the SUV.

Bryg looked over his shoulder and saw Leah had remained inside, though her stare was firmly on Zeke.

"You brought her." Zeke gave a husky laugh.

"She's worried about you. Everyone is," Bryg said.

"How d'you know where to find me?" Zeke gave him a curious look.

"I grew up here," Bryg said. When Zeke's eyes widened, Bryg gave a dry laugh. "I'll tell you about it someday. How'd you get here so fast?"

"A bunch of kids in a pickup gave me a ride."

Bryg nodded, then laid a hand on Zeke's shoulder and turned him toward the SUV.

Zeke stiffened and Bryg waited for the argument—that Zeke didn't want to go back. That he wanted to stay in The Grid. This was where he belonged.

"They said I smelled funny. That I smelled like a ranch." Zeke was shaking. The threat of tears climbed into his voice.

"Different maybe, but not funny." Bryg wished Zeke realized his old friends probably didn't know what a ranch smelled like.

He had a feeling Zeke's friends probably said a few other things. What Zeke didn't understand was that his friends were probably jealous. His clothes were different, and maybe he smelled different, but it would've been the scent of the country, and not the inner city.

A tear rolled down Zeke's cheek. He uttered an oath and wiped it away.

"It's okay," Bryg said, his voice rough.

Zeke was a kid who kept a lot inside. He needed to let go—of his emotions and of The Grid.

The boy rolled his eyes and looked away, a determined effort to keep from crying.

Bryg understood. He used to think crying was a sign of weakness. Now he knew—it took strength to cry.

"You hungry?" Bryg asked him.

Zeke looked surprised, then dropped his gaze. "Yeah."

"Let's get something to eat." Bryg wrapped his arm around Zeke's shoulder and guided him to the SUV. "I've got a few snacks in the car, but we'll stop at a restaurant and get you some real food."

When they approached the SUV, Leah climbed out. Her face was pale, but her full lips spread into a smile that made Bryg's heart rise in his chest. When he saw the sheen in her eyes, his throat dried.

"Hi, Zeke," she said when he and Bryg were a few feet away from her. Her voice almost sounded normal.

"Hi." Zeke gave her a tentative smile, as if expecting more than just a greeting.

"I told him we'd get something to eat," Bryg said. He opened the SUV's back door and helped Zeke inside.

Leah nodded and climbed into the car. She leaned over the back of the seat and handed the bag with snacks to Zeke. Bryg slid into the driver's seat and started the engine. He felt a stare and looked at the row of houses set back from the sidewalk. He glanced at the homes, all with tiny front porches. All with the shades pulled down tight. Movement on the second floor of one house caught his attention, and he wondered who watched. One of Zeke's friends? The one who told Zeke he smelled like a ranch?

The one who wished he smelled like a ranch?

Bryg pulled away from the curb. If that was what the kid wanted, Bryg hoped it would happen.

The sense of relief flooding Bryg now was almost his undoing. He prayed for the kid who had hurt Zeke, and he murmured a prayer of thanks.

He and Leah had found Zeke. He glanced into the rearview mirror and caught Zeke's profile as he stared at the tiny brick houses they passed. His features had relaxed, and it was the first time Bryg had looked into his young face and not seen resentment.

Tension drained out of Bryg's chest when they reached the boulevard and headed toward the highway. His throat felt raw as he remembered how he'd fought the social service workers the day they'd dragged him out of the studio apartment he'd shared with his mother.

She was crying, too, and said she'd visit him, but she never did. Was that Zeke's story? He hadn't gone to a house or an apartment. Because he didn't have one to go to? Did he have a family? Were they still alive?

Bryg glanced at Leah and breathed a little easier when he saw the lines around her mouth and eyes had eased.

Reaching over, he squeezed her hand. She looked at him, but didn't seem surprised. She laid a hand over his and tightened her slender fingers around his. He felt her warmth, felt the smoothness of her skin. Briefly, he wondered if Zeke noticed this exchange between Bryg and Leah, but he didn't care.

He didn't want to release Leah, but slowly he slid his hand away from hers. The longing he felt inside made him want to wrap her in his arms and hold her close, inhale the fragrance of her skin that made him long for something more.

And in that moment, he knew she was the woman he wanted to hold for a very long time.

CHAPTER 9

*F*our days later, Leah and her parents sat in the dining room and stared at the drawings spread across the table.

Bryg had stopped by the house every day to let them know the progress with the drawings. Sometimes, he stayed for dinner. He always played baseball or touch football with the boys. That Zeke had lost his sullen attitude and joined the fun was refreshing and a relief.

When Leah would walk Bryg to his car afterward, she felt so comfortable—as if he were part of the family, but caution loomed nearby, and Leah kept the conversations casual. One heartbreak had proved one too many. She wouldn't let her desire to grow closer to Bryg lead her to something she felt too fragile to endure.

Now, she stood next to the dining room table and looked at Bryg's drawings. She swallowed. Colorful images of brick homes with three and four car garages filled the table-sized sheets, their curled corners anchored with glasses and vases. Rolled and rubber-banded drawings of the commercial plans stood in the corner.

Bryg stood next to Leah and explained the ideas that would become a reality as soon as her parents signed the sales contract. She couldn't ignore Bryg's pleasant voice, his relaxed and in-charge posture, his masculine scent.

Saying little, she listened to the plans that should've made her excited. Instead, she felt something sliding through her fingers—it was the ranch, and she wasn't ready to let it go.

Until she left for college, the ranch was the only home she'd known. She always thought she'd spend the holidays and summer breaks here. After she and Charlie married, they'd bring their children here.

What children? That dream had disintegrated. She didn't miss Charlie. Her throat dried whenever she thought of the plans they'd made—the cute house in a quiet neighborhood, the miniature collie racing around their feet, the two-point-two children toddling across the lawn. She'd even chosen names for their children and the dog. Why had she never suspected Charlie's interest in someone else?

Why hadn't he told her?

"It looks like you'll have a real nice community here." Vern looked down at the drawings, then looked up at Bryg. He smiled with his mouth, but not with his eyes.

Leah knew Bryg hadn't missed the forced encouragement in her father's voice.

Her mother sat next to her husband and nodded. She said nothing, but her hands clasped on the tabletop spoke volumes.

Outside, the boys played baseball in the yard next to the barn in the unseasonably warm December afternoon. They called to each other. The crack of a bat hitting the ball sounded, and the boys' voices rose, Zeke's being the loudest of all. Since he'd returned to the ranch, he'd seemed more relaxed, talked more, and even helped Carl with his homework. Zeke was a whiz in math and always had a bookmark in a paperback.

He was also intuitive and didn't miss that things were changing at the ranch.

Her parents had told the boys they might sell the ranch, but nothing would change as long as the boys lived here. Frankie and Zeke would graduate the spring after next. Harry and Carl the following spring. That seemed to reassure the boys, but they still asked a lot of questions.

Leah knew her parents needed to retire. They'd worked hard and deserved a break, even if it meant living in a condo in Florida.

"My staff is working on some other ideas. I'll have them overnight the plans today, and we can discuss them tomorrow." The tone in Bryg's voice didn't change. The enthusiasm was still strong, but his eyes showed he hadn't missed the hesitancy weighing over Leah and her parents.

"I don't think we need any more ideas." Leah's father leaned back in his chair and waved his hand over the drawings. "I can't imagine anything being nicer than what you have here."

"There's always room for improvement." Bryg smiled at him.

Leah released a soft breath. Bryg was trying so hard to prove to them the community would be family oriented. The emptiness scratching the inside of her chest wouldn't relieve the doubt that no matter what he presented, the new community wouldn't be the Mardale she loved.

"When are we going to get a Christmas tree?" Zeke stood in the doorway between the dining room and the kitchen. He was breathing hard and his damp hair curled in a smooth cap over his well-shaped head. Three eager faces peered around him.

"How about now?" Leah's father looked at his wife then Leah then Bryg. "I hope you don't mind. We promised the boys we'd get the tree today. You're welcome to come with us."

"I'd like that," Bryg said. The light shining in Bryg's eyes warmed Leah's heart, but also made her a little sad because she had a feeling he hadn't decorated a Christmas tree in a very long time.

She should know. The only tree she decorated was the one they had at the ranch each year. She'd never had her own Christmas tree, because she always spent the holiday with her family.

"Where do you buy the Christmas tree?" A frown pressed into Bryg's forehead, as if he were trying to remember where he'd seen the town's Christmas tree lot.

"We don't," Leah said with a soft laugh. "We grow them on the ranch. People come from all over to buy one of ours. It's the thrill of chopping down your own tree and taking it back to your home."

Bryg arched his brow.

"I take it, you've never chopped down your own tree," Leah said.

"No, but there's a first time for everything," he said and smiled. He rolled up the drawings and scooped up the others standing in the corner. "I'll put these in the car and be right back."

When he returned, the boys were bundled. They burst out the back door, eager for freedom and an adventure. Leah's father carried an ax and led the group down a hard-packed trail to a grove of trees tucked behind the barn. The boys' voices rose as they raced through the even rows and inspected each tree. Leah didn't miss the interest in Bryg's eyes as he watched the boys move from tree to tree before finally reaching a consensus. Their eyes bright, their bodies electrified, they pointed to one that would fit nicely in the living room at the base of the stairs.

"You sure that's the one?" Leah's father said, and he slid the ax from its case.

The boys' eyes went wide, and they watched his every move.

"I'm happy to do the honors, if you like," Bryg said quietly, but it got the boys' attention.

"Be my guest." Vern handed him the ax.

Bryg held it in his gloved hands and swung it against the tree trunk, his broad shoulders working beneath his jacket.

"Timber," the boys yelled as the tree crashed to the ground. They rushed to pick it up. Balancing it on their shoulders, they marched back to the house.

In the dining room, Leah set stacks of colored construction paper, glue and containers of glitter for the boys to create Christmas decorations. While they worked, she and her mother popped a bowl of popcorn and cooked cocoa for the boys whose eyes stretched wide when they saw the treats.

In the living room, her mother set out a box filled with Christmas decorations while Bryg worked with Leah's father to set up the tree.

Leah only glanced at Bryg helping her father before she set mugs filled with cocoa and marshmallows in front of each boy, but the image of Bryg in the living room etched into her mind. How appropriate it felt having Bryg here and helping her family decorate the house for the holiday.

She pulled a chair next to Zeke and showed him how to cut the construction paper in strips and glue the ends together to make a chain. She had to do something so she wouldn't gawk at Bryg, his handsome face, his magnificent build. That he seemed interested in helping the family prepare for the Christmas celebration was a warning she couldn't ignore. She had to remember he was here for her father's approval of the development. As the mayor, the community looked to her father for guidance. If Bryg convinced her father the development would preserve the small town charm, then the ranch owners in the area would follow her father's lead.

"What do you think of this?" Zeke held up a colorful chain. Silver and gold and red and green glitter gleamed over the loops.

"That's beautiful," Leah exclaimed. A softness filled her at the pleased look in Zeke's eyes.

How many boys had her parents guided to believe in themselves and become contributing members of society? Her chest squeezed. She hated the thought that this would be the last group. After these boys left, her parents would leave the ranch. Leah would return to Braxton. The meadows stretching across the rolling hills would be plowed and become neighborhoods where families would live, work and play.

Would that be so bad? She'd always been in favor of change.

By the end of the afternoon, the tree glittered and sparkled with the boys' homemade decorations. Boughs clung to the staircase bannister. Stockings with each boy's name hung above the fireplace. Her mother had even made a stocking for Bryg.

Surprise flickered in Bryg's eyes. His voice was husky when he thanked Leah's mother.

"Not that we expect you to stay. The house will be full because our son and his family drive up from Texas. Besides, I'm sure you already have plans," Mavis said, when she hung the stocking over the fireplace. "But you're welcome to celebrate here, if you like."

"Thank you," Bryg said, and looked at Leah, a question in his eyes.

Leah took in a quick breath. He wanted to accept, but his decision lay with her.

"I think it would be wonderful to have you join us," she said, the words spilling out before she realized what they meant—Bryg would spend Christmas day with her, and everyone else in the family. "Of course, if you've already made plans ..."

"I don't have any plans," he said.

That gave Leah a start. Bryg had to have dozens of friends who'd want to celebrate the holiday with him. She wouldn't think about the girlfriends.

"I'd be honored to spend the holiday with you." Bryg looked at the boys. "With all of you."

The boys gave shouts of approval, then turned back to the cardboard box filled with Christmas decorations.

From inside, Leah's mother lifted tissue wrapped packages. She checked the labels on each one, then handed them to the boys. Surprised at first, they ripped through the paper and pulled out tiny picture frames that held photos of each boy. The boys looked at the frames in awe and wonder.

"These are yours," her mother explained. "You can put them on the tree or keep them. It's your choice."

Each boy hung his picture on the tree, except Zeke. He held his, and everyone waited quietly. When he hooked the ribbon over a branch, the other boys relaxed.

With the tree decorated, Leah's parents invited Bryg to stay for the dinner. Afterward, Leah and her parents settled the boys into their rooms to start homework, then Leah's father announced he'd check on the animals.

"I'll do that, Dad," Leah said. Her opportunities to check on the animals would soon end. She'd take advantage of every moment she had.

"Do you want some company?" Bryg's gaze rested on her in his gentle but decidedly unsettling way.

"That would be nice," she said, before she could think better about it, but Bryg was quickly becoming part of the family. His charm and concern drew people to him—including Leah.

Once the ranch sold, she'd never see Bryg again. A hollowness rose inside her, but she pushed it down. Not seeing Bryg wouldn't be the same as when she broke her engagement to Charlie. She and Charlie had dated for two years before he proposed. She barely knew Bryg, so what she felt couldn't be love. The only thing between her and Bryg was like, and Bryg was a very likable guy.

Leah and Bryg walked past the pigpen, and the pigs grunted softly .

Suddenly, a loud squeal erupted. Annoyed grunts followed. Leah stood at the edge of the yard and looked into the pen.

One pig rose on her hind legs and rested her front feet against the middle rail.

Babe.

She'd grown bigger, heavier, and maybe more vocal in the nearly two weeks that had passed.

Leah hated ignoring the pig, but she kept her distance. It hurt too much to become attached to an animal that would soon be shipped to market.

"I take it, that's Babe." Bryg's warm breath was soft against her hair.

"Yes," Leah said, a tremor in her voice.

"Come on." Bryg's fingers wrapped around hers and took a step toward the barn.

She lifted her gaze to his, to eyes dark with concern. The warmth of his touch filled her with a comfort she'd never felt when Charlie took her hand.

"I hate ignoring her," Leah said and fell into step beside Bryg.

The pig's squeals faded when they stepped inside the barn, but it didn't ease the regret rising inside Leah. If she could take Babe back to the college with her, she would, but it would be hard to pretend a five hundred pound pig was an ordinary pet.

Inside the barn, she checked the horses, though the boys and her father would have already freshened their feed and water.

Leah scooped apples from the barrel and moved to a palomino's stall door. She held the apple to the horse, who gracefully worked the fruit into her mouth.

What would happen to all these animals when her parents sold the ranch? The thought brought a lump to her throat. They were like family to her.

Quick tears pricked her eyes.

"Hey," Bryg's husky voice broke through the emotions she could barely rein in.

His touch tentative, he slid his hand down her arm. Gently, so gently, he pulled her close until her body pressed into the solid ridged muscles of his chest. She closed her eyes and drank in the feel of him, his scent sweet and spicy at once.

"It never occurred to me a day would come when the animals wouldn't be here anymore." Her throat closed at the crack running through her heart. "I always knew I was fortunate to have this life, but I still took it for granted."

"So what would it take for you to understand that Mardale will still maintain its country charm?" Bryg touched a finger to her chin and tipped her gaze to his.

"I don't think there's anything you can do," she said with a dry laugh. "All your plans show that everything about the ranch will be preserved. The commercial areas will maintain the quaintness of the town. I just need to let go."

"You can always come back." He spoke so sincerely, Leah couldn't doubt him, but what would she come back to? Her parents would be gone.

She looked into eyes that seemed to want to fix whatever bothered her. How could Bryg Winslow, who would have multiple business transactions going on at the same time, spend so much time on this project?

"Why is this project so important to you?" she asked. Bryg had to be the most confusing and alluring man she'd ever met.

"I've asked myself that question a few times." He brushed his knuckles against her cheek.

Such a tender touch that brought unwanted emotions to the surface. She looked into his eyes. Compassion and longing shone there, unhidden. Something rose within her that could almost match what she saw in Bryg's eyes.

"You have no idea what a temptation you are right now," he said and took in a deep breath.

Leah's throat dried. "I didn't mean——"

"I know you didn't." He laughed softly. "Which makes you so refreshing." He lifted his gaze to the rafters before looking at her again. "Normally, I've been good at keeping my emotions out of my business dealings, but with you, I failed miserably."

Her eyes stretched wide, and her heart kicked up a notch. She'd never expected any man to make such a confession, let alone charming and polished Bryg Winslow. She knew she should put distance between them, but she couldn't bear to not feel the softness and affection of this powerful man.

"I don't know what to say." Leah could barely form the words.

"I'm a little stunned myself." Bryg gave a soft snort. "I don't know what it is about you, but it's been difficult to hide my feelings when I'm around you."

"You hardly know me." She blinked and blushed.

"Here's something really crazy," he said and looked into her eyes. "I feel like I've known you for a very long time."

She said nothing. His words echoed inside her head.

"When this is all over, I'd like to get to know you better. Hopefully, you'll agree, and don't look at me like this is a line," he said.

"I didn't mean …" She couldn't finish. She stifled a gasp. How had he known what she'd been thinking? Was she that transparent. "I'd like that … Getting to know each other."

And if he changed his mind? Her life would be no different. Until two weeks ago, she would never have guessed Bryg Winslow would step into her life.

"Maybe we should get back," he said, the hesitancy in his voice reflecting the reluctance in her heart.

Nodding, she drew back. She longed to stay in his arms, but things were moving too fast with the development negotiations and these feelings between her and Bryg. She'd known Charlie for a year before they went on their first date.

"I'll say goodbye to your parents," he said. "I'll talk to my staff when I drive back to the house tonight and discuss some changes we can make that will appeal to your parents."

"You'll call your staff tonight?" She couldn't hide the surprise in her voice. "And why make changes? My parents never said they wanted any."

"True, but I'm one who never stops until everything is perfect."

"That, I believe," she said with a laugh. "But why tonight? If you want to wait until tomorrow, we can wait another day."

"I'd like to get the ideas finalized while they're still fresh in my mind." He extended his hand to her.

She put her hand in his and let him lead her from the barn. Their conversation moved from the ranch to life in Mardale until they entered the house. Inside, Bryg thanked her parents for the hospitality and said he'd call them tomorrow and explained he had some new ideas he wanted to present to them. Leah walked him out the front door to his SUV. He told her to go inside, but she couldn't leave him. Not yet.

Instead, she huddled in her coat and waited until he drove away.

The SUV's taillights disappeared over the horizon, but Leah didn't move. She tried to understand the turn her life had taken since returning home two weeks ago. She had thought her life had crumbled when she'd walked into Charlie's office and found him entangled with his assistant.

Now, she was falling for a man she'd never imagined she'd meet, let alone have feelings for. She pressed her gloved hands to her lips. Things were happening too fast. She had seen pictures of the women Bryg dated, and she was nothing like them. And when Bryg confessed his feelings for her, she believed him. Was she a fool? Nothing about her feelings for Bryg made sense. She needed to take a step back and analyze what was happening here.

Bryg Winslow was about to change her life. Once the ranch sold, she'd never have a place to come back to for Christmas, for summer vacations, for anything.

And suddenly she realized she wasn't willing to let that happen.

The only problem was that this wasn't her decision to make.

CHAPTER 10

*L*eah could barely sleep that night, crawling out of bed several times to stare out the window at the sky filled with the stars she couldn't see when she was at her home in Massachusetts.

Even before the alarm went off, she was out of bed, dressed and downstairs. In the kitchen, she found her mother's weekly grocery list and added a few items. She'd shop after breakfast. Keeping busy was the best thing for her to do while her parents worked through finalizing the ranch sale with Bryg.

She swallowed her disappointment and pulled pans from the cupboard. Making breakfast should get her mind off what was about to happen, but thoughts of the coming changes edged into her mind. She chided herself that her thoughts centered around herself. The ranch belonged to her parents. Life at the ranch was the priceless gift they had given her.

When her mother stepped into the kitchen, Leah chatted but saw the knowing look in her mother's eyes——Leah couldn't hide the disappointment piercing her heart. After her father took the boys to the barn, Leah told her mother she'd take care of the shopping and dashed out to the family truck.

At the town co-op, Leah filled a cart with items and greeted friends, but always the conversation drifted to the new development. Some people were excited. Others were concerned.

In the produce department, Leah saw Holly Johnson, the widow who owned the ranch next door to her family ranch. There was a sadness in Holly's eyes when Leah greeted her.

"I feel badly I want to sell," Holly said, and Leah gave up trying to talk to friends and neighbors about anything except the development. "I feel like I started something."

"You're doing what's right for you." Leah took her hand, though the ache in her friend's eyes weighed heavy in her heart.

Holly and her husband never had children. The ranch was too much for a single woman to manage.

"I try to tell myself that," Holly said, "When I spoke to the real estate broker, I thought he'd find a family who would want to take it over. I never expected some New York billionaire to be interested in a place that isn't even a dot on the map."

Leah held her breath. "What if a family did want to buy your ranch? Would you change your mind?" She didn't know why she asked that. She didn't know anyone who wanted to buy a ranch out on the plains. Everyone she knew lived in the city. Sometimes her friends vacationed in the country, but they loved the city.

So did she.

"In a minute," Holly said with a weak laugh. "But who wants to live in Mardale? Kids who grew up here couldn't wait to leave." She looked at Leah.

Leah swallowed. It wasn't that she had wanted to leave Mardale. She loved this quaint town and the folksy residents who went out of their way to say hello and always had time to chat. If she hadn't received a scholarship to one of the best colleges in the country, she'd still be here. Maybe she would've married one of the boys in her class, though she didn't know who. None of the boys had interested her. When she received the scholarship, she knew she couldn't miss the opportunity to pursue her education, but it had never occurred to her she'd only visit Mardale. She wouldn't live here.

"What if someone wanted to buy the ranch and keep it as a ranch?" Leah asked, her voice hesitant. Who would that be?

"If you know someone, send them my way." Holly gave a cheerless laugh under her breath. "But make it soon. I've got some decisions to make. I hate being the one who sells out to a developer, but I hear others talking. We're all getting too old to ranch, and Mr. Winslow is making offers none of us ever imagined, but I guess you know that because he's talking to your dad."

Leah nodded and curved the corner of her mouth. Talk of selling the ranch made her realize nothing lasted forever. Of course, she'd learned that when she'd walked in on Charlie. She forced a smile at Holly. She didn't want her friend to be sad and said she needed to pay for her groceries before the ice cream melted.

The price Bryg had offered Leah's parents was what Leah had paid for her condo near the Braxton campus, which was located in a posh section of the town.

Her heart swelled. If she could afford that condo, she could afford to buy the ranch. When she and Charlie were discussing where they'd live after they married, he had mentioned her condo was now worth twice what she'd paid for it. She'd almost choked on her shrimp cocktail. He had said that to her a year ago. What would it be worth now?

She anchored the groceries into the truck bed, but her mind wouldn't stop working. When she returned to the ranch, she'd call a real estate friend of hers in Boston. Not that she would sell her condo. She had to live somewhere, but it would be interesting to know the value. She wouldn't stay at Braxton forever.

But when she left Braxton, she wouldn't return to Mardale. Her jaw tightened. Where would she go? To Florida?

She couldn't wait until she returned to the ranch and called her friend when she drove out of the co-op parking lot.

"I'm so glad you called," her friend said after she and Leah wished each other Merry Christmas. "The new prof in the music department is looking for something near the campus, and after he sees what you've done to the place, he'll fall in love. I'll send you some information on the sales in the area and then we can discuss an asking price.

Leah almost choked. "I'm not sure I want to sell."

"No problem. It's always good to know the local market," her friend said, and Leah heard a tapping sound as if her friend typed on a computer keyboard. "That house you and Charlie were considering is still on the market."

Leah exhaled roughly. Apparently, not everyone knew she and Charlie had ended their engagement.

"Thanks, I'll keep it in mind," she said, and hoped she sounded grateful.

When her friend told her what she could ask for her condo, Leah almost drove off the road. Almost twice what Bryg had offered her parents for their ranch. Leah tried to take a breath. How could a two thousand square foot condominium have more value than a few hundred acres of land?

Before Leah and her friend ended the call, Leah said she'd be in touch. She barely remembered driving back to the ranch.

A turmoil of thoughts plunged through her mind. If she sold her condominium, she'd almost have enough money to buy Holly's ranch and her parents' ranch.

That gave her a start. What would she do with two ranches? Could she qualify for a mortgage?

And where would she live in Braxton? Then there was the foster home. She couldn't live in Braxton and raise foster children. They'd need a father figure, which would make the job better suited for a couple. She couldn't see Charlie as a foster parent, and she shouldn't be thinking about him anyway. He was no longer a part of her life.

Someone like Bryg would make a good foster parent. She closed her eyes and shook her head. What was she thinking? Bryg was a wealthy man who negotiated business deals. He wouldn't walk away from the corporation he built to care for unwanted boys. Never mind that he'd been one of those boys more than twenty years ago.

But Bryg hadn't forgotten his roots. He helped her look for Zeke. Thanks to his street smarts, they'd found the boy, but the corporation he ran was sophisticated and intricate. He was one of the most eligible bachelors in the country, probably the world. He'd worked hard and built an empire. He'd never walk away from that.

And why was she even thinking of him as a foster parent? She laughed weakly. She'd only known him for a few weeks. He'd said he wanted to get to know her better, but that didn't mean he'd consider a future with her. She had a great career, and she'd focus on that.

If she sold her condo to buy her parents' and the Johnson ranch, teaching at Braxton would be impossible if she lived in Mardale.

Unless she held her classes online. She could live anywhere. Several faculty members taught online courses, and many of them did not live in Massachusetts. She'd miss the face-to-face contact with her students, but she could still travel to Braxton for occasional lectures and events.

She picked up the phone. The first thing she had to do was find out if the college would let her teach online. If they did, the details of her plan would fall into place—except for the foster home, but she wouldn't give up yet.

LEAH HAD JUST FINISHED her conversation with the dean of the English department, when Bryg arrived at the house that afternoon.

When she told the dean she'd like to teach online, he'd told her it was too late to change her status for the winter and spring quarters, but the department would consider her request for the fall. That disappointed Leah, but she wouldn't give up. She'd make her plan work.

Bryg's SUV coasted down the gravel driveway and parked in front of the farmhouse.

Leah stood in front of the upstairs bedroom window and sensed his excitement before he stepped out of the SUV. Setting her jaw, she turned away. She didn't want to spy on him, but not wanting to watch this powerfully built man was like visiting the Grand Canyon and keeping your eyes closed.

The boys were in their rooms working on their assignments when

Leah and her parents sat around the dining room table and stared at the laptop Bryg set in front of them. The video playing across the screen showed the subtle segue from ranch to residential and commercial centers. Everything about the development carefully maintained the ranch town. The greenways bordering the residential areas and the commercial campuses still looked like the flower-filled pastures where horses and cattle grazed.

When the video faded to a logo of the Winslow Corporation, Leah's parents leaned back in their chairs and looked at each other.

Leah released a slow breath. The video showed everything she and her parents wanted. The town and surrounding spreads would be preserved. The residential and commercial areas blended well with the town and ranches. Quaint Mardale would keep its country feeling.

"I like it," her father said in his folksy way. "I'll call the city council and set up a meeting with the members." His mouth curved, and he looked at Bryg. "Of course, Mavis and I are not leaving until the last of these boys has graduated high school and has a job or will start college."

"I fully agree," Bryg said. His face kind and understanding. If he felt the victory of the conquering hero, he hid it well. "We can start the preliminary work. When you're ready to finalize the sale, everything will be in place."

"What if one of the ranch owners received another offer?" Leah asked. She hadn't meant to say anything. She couldn't sell her condo, and she couldn't buy her parents' ranch, let alone Holly's ranch until she could teach her winter and spring courses online. Until the college agreed, that wasn't possible. Though her real estate friend had a buyer for her condo, she still had to qualify for a loan for her parents' ranch and the Johnson ranch. Other ranches would be on the market, but she couldn't buy the valley. She wasn't Bryg Winslow.

"Do you know of another offer?" Bryg asked, the surprise in his eyes vanished, and his corporate persona slid into place.

"I don't have details." Was that a lie? She didn't know if she'd qualify for the loan, so maybe it wasn't. Qualifying for a loan was an important detail. "But it's possible someone else might be interested in a couple of the ranches." Leah released a slow breath. With three pairs of curious gazes on her, she wished she'd said nothing.

"Might this other interested party be you?" Bryg asked with no inflection in his voice, as though he spoke to a business associate.

Leah's breath caught, and she pushed the feelings she had for Bryg deep down inside her.

No longer was he the man she had fought to protect her heart from. Her pulse jumped wildly. She now looked into the keen eyes of a master negotiator.

CHAPTER 11

*L*eah stared into Bryg's brilliant blue eyes that never wavered from hers. She heard her mother gasp and felt her father stiffen, but didn't look at them. Bryg's question left no room for her to dance around the truth.

"Yes," she said finally, "I've scheduled an appointment to talk to the local banker about qualifying for a mortgage for my parents' ranch and the Johnson ranch."

She should've expected Bryg's calm demeanor at her admission. He was far too composed and experienced to show his emotions. In his dealings, he would've conducted business with all kinds of nego- tiators. Leah's business acumen wouldn't come close to his.

He remained quiet. Leah knew it was because she would feel oblig- ated to fill the stillness with an explanation. If she were to have any inner peace, she'd have to tell him and her parents everything.

"Leah, why?" Her mother broke through the silence.

"I'm not ready for this valley to change." She never stopped looking at Bryg.

He didn't move. He just looked at her and waited.

"You've done so much good with the boys who come here every year." Tension coiled in her stomach. She broke her gaze from Bryg and looked at her parents. "I realize that you've decided it's time you step back. This is a job for a young person. I've always been proud of what you've done with these boys. I always appreciated what you did for David and me. There are other boys that will need the same guidance, and I'd like to provide that to them."

"How? You have your teaching position back east." Her mother's face knitted with mounting confusion.

"I haven't worked out all the details." She wouldn't share that the dean of the English department hadn't agreed to her proposal that she teach online classes until the fall—if then. "But I'm hoping that by the time you're ready to leave, I'll have everything in place."

"You'll need a partner," Bryg said. "A father figure is important for boys, especially boys who need precise guidance."

"I've thought of that," Leah said and tried to keep her voice steady.

Bryg had been one of those boys. He knew what they needed. Bryg had received the guidance he needed. That combined with his intelligence and drive helped create the empire he now ran.

Would Charlie have compassion for boys like Zeke and Frankie and Bryg? She wouldn't change her mind about breaking her engagement to Charlie. She hadn't returned his messages, though she knew she should. What he had done still made her heart ache, but she could forgive him. Forgiveness gave her freedom, and made her grateful, because she realized *before* they married, he wasn't the man for her.

Charlie loved his reputation as topnotch lawyer at a prestigious law firm. He'd never sacrifice that to raise boys in need. During their engagement, he'd never discussed starting a family. She had, and he simply nodded and smiled as if he found her endearing and amusing.

"You have someone to partner with to help raise boys in need of a home?" Bryg's business persona seemed to slip, as if he realized there was someone in her life that could step into that position.

"Not exactly," she said slowly. "I'm working on some ideas. Can you give me a few days to see if I can make this work?" She looked at her parents.

"Honey, you can have as long as you want." Her mother took her hand and gave it a gentle squeeze.

"We're not going anywhere," her father said. "We made a commitment to these boys, and we're here as long as they're here." Her father gave a rough exhale. Whatever he thought of her buying their ranch and Holly's ranch, he'd keep to himself.

Leah knew what settled deep in her father's heart. When these boys left, her parents would no longer have boys to lead and guide.

"I've called the foster parent agency. They have a list of couples who would like to foster boys. They understand you'll raise the boys here now, but when you leave, they'll place a couple to take over the care of the next group of boys until I can take …" When would she take over? The agency worked with couples. She had no prospects of being a couple with anyone. "The couple would have experience working a ranch and would parent the boys until they graduated high school."

"You've been busy," Bryg said.

"I'm sorry," she said, her voice thin. When she looked at him, the guilt rising in her throat made her choke.

Bryg had worked hard to make the development appealing to the community. Because her father was the town mayor, Bryg had made certain her father approved everything. Once plans were finalized, Bryg would present his proposal to the community at a town hall.

She looked at her parents. "And I owe you apologies, too. Everyone's worked so hard to make the development work." She swallowed. "If it weren't for me, it would have."

"Honey." Her mother patted her hand. "We don't blame you for anything."

"This is a business deal," Bryg said, his tone sincere. "I can't deny I like a challenge. If there weren't a chance the townsfolk wouldn't agree to my ideas, I probably wouldn't work as hard as I do."

Leah felt hot with embarrassment. "So you're not walking away from this development?" She looked at him wide-eyed, panic setting in.

"This time, I will walk away." Amazing how calm he sounded. Leah had a feeling he'd never walked away before. "I see how much this means to you. You've seen the good your parents have accomplished with this home, and you want it to continue." He waited a moment. "And I think it should." He powered down his laptop.

"You're leaving?" Leah's pulse skyrocketed. She knew how much he wanted to develop Mardale. He reworked the plan three times. No one would do that if he didn't want the place.

"I hope to be back, but maybe under different circumstances." His eyes were so clear, she couldn't misunderstand what he meant. He'd come back for her? Why? She was interfering with his plans.

And he didn't seem to care that her parents were sitting right here. They said nothing and didn't act as if what Bryg said was unusual.

Leah swallowed hard. Different circumstances meant something between him and Leah. Her heart felt as if it would crack. She was attracted to Bryg. Who wouldn't be? This strongly built man had a compassion she'd never felt in another man, but it would be a long time, if ever, that she could trust her heart to someone else. Sorrow rose up from deep inside her. The scar of a broken engagement ran deep.

Bryg slipped his laptop into its sleeve and rose.

Talk to him. Her voice shouted inside her head. She was so dizzy she wanted to fall back into her chair. Instead, she grabbed the corner of the table.

What should she say? Stay for dinner? That would be awkward, especially after she'd destroyed the plan he'd worked so hard to design.

"I don't suppose you want to stay for dinner." Leah couldn't believe she had the nerve to ask him. Her voice was so soft, she wasn't sure he heard her.

He looked at her. His slight smile didn't match the intensity in his eyes. "I would, except I have to meet one of my teams in Boise. If I fly there tonight, it will give us a chance to work through some things before our meeting with the city council tomorrow."

"The boys ..." She closed her eyes and shook her head. Her heart sank into the pit of her stomach. She couldn't bring the boys into this. Yes, they'd miss Bryg, but they weren't his responsibility.

"I'll say goodbye to them," he said, as if that had been his plan.

Doors opening and closing sounded from upstairs. Had the boys finished their schoolwork? Footsteps moved down the stairs.

"Christmas ..." Leah said hoarsely. Why was she speaking mono-syllabically? She was a professor! Speech was her life. She waved her hand, dismissing what she'd said. He had said he'd like to spend Christmas here, but now? Probably not so much.

"You're leaving, aren't you?" Zeke stood on the bottom step, his wide-eyed stare at Bryg making Leah's throat squeeze tight.

Frankie and the other boys stood behind him, their mouths slack.

"Unfortunately, but I'll be back," Bryg said. He stepped to the stairs and gripped each boy's hand.

It looked like goodbye. From the look on the boys' faces, they knew. How many people had walked out of their lives? Too many, but the number didn't matter because they'd never get used to it.

Bryg was leaving, and it was Leah's fault.

"When?" Zeke asked, challenge in his eyes.

"As soon as I can," Bryg said. His mouth firmed as if he regretted being vague, but he didn't say if he'd be back for Christmas.

That was Leah's fault, too.

"Promise me, you'll keep up with your schoolwork." Bryg arched a brow at Zeke, then looked at the other boys.

"I will." Frankie wiggled his shoulders. "I'm the smartest one here."

"You are not." Carl's voice rose.

Harry said something Leah didn't understand, which may have been a good thing.

Zeke remained silent and stared at Bryg, defiance on his face.

"You're all smart, and I'll check in with Mavis and Vern to see how smart you are," Bryg said and tipped his head toward the door. "Walk me out to the car?"

Frankie and the other boys pushed past Zeke, almost knocking him over, and plastered themselves to Bryg while he shook hands with Leah's father and hugged Mavis. Leah envied the boys their release of emotions but didn't miss that Zeke remained on the stairs.

Bryg's gaze settled on Leah in that warm and comforting way he had that made everyone he met feel like the most important person in the world. Except Leah didn't feel important. She looked into Bryg's brilliant blue eyes but knew the boys watched her. She felt awkward beneath their intense stares.

She remained still. She wanted to rush into Bryg's arms and hold him close. The boys watched as if they expected her to do just that.

Bryg stepped to Zeke and held out his hand. Zeke stared at it, then flung his arms round Bryg's neck. The emotion rising in the boy's throat caught on Leah's heart like a ragged corner. She was prying Bryg out of these boys' lives. As quickly as Zeke hugged Bryg, he released him. He wiped at his eyes with the back of his roughened hand.

'Bye," Zeke said, his tone husky.

"It isn't goodbye." Bryg's voice was soft and firm. "I'll be back, and that's a promise."

As if afraid to speak, Zeke could only nod.

Everyone walked out with Bryg. Zeke waited a moment and followed. Leah followed him.

When Bryg drove away, he stuck an arm out the window and waved, the rear tires kicking up gravel and snow. The boys waved with Zeke waiting a moment before he waved. Leah's parents waved.

Leah waved.

"Let's check on the animals," Leah's father said. He tipped his head and walked toward the barn. The boys followed him.

Zeke stared after Bryg's car, then turned and followed the others. He hesitated in front of Leah, the look in his eyes telling her Bryg would be back. She smiled at Zeke. She believed that, too.

Bryg was a man of his word. If only his leaving didn't make her heart crack in two.

CHAPTER 12

*L*eah sat in the office of the Mardale bank's vice president, Isaac Lewis, and gave him a stunned look. "What do you mean I'm a financial risk? My condo is worth almost as much as the Johnson and my parents' ranch combined. I have a good job."

"Let's start with the condo. It's mortgaged, so you don't own it outright. After you sell, you'll have to pay off the mortgage," Isaac explained patiently. "As for your job, you haven't worked there long enough to prove you're not a financial risk."

"I've been there for six years." Leah forced a calm she didn't feel into her voice.

"But not as an associate professor. You said you would switch your status to an online position, which could mean a reduced salary."

Leah's breath caught. Was that why the dean hadn't agreed to her teaching remotely? He had mentioned nothing about reducing her income. She was counting on her salary and future pay raises to cover ranch expenses, which would be high. If she hired a couple to continue with the foster care, she'd pay them a salary, and the general care for the boys wouldn't be cheap.

Lord, what had I been thinking? Her face went hot with humiliation. She hadn't been thinking, and she hadn't sought the Lord's guidance.

"If the college agrees to your teaching online, we'll contact them for salary confirmation," Isaac said, his voice pleasant but not encouraging.

"I have a pension. I could cash that in." Her mind whirled. There had to be a way to make this work.

"I wouldn't advise it." Isaac looked at her over the top of his glasses.

"There has to be a way to make this work." She bit her lip.

"Maybe you should forget about it until after the holidays." Isaac gave her a sympathetic look. "A new year. A new outlook on life. We can set up a meeting ..."

She didn't hear the rest of what he said. Nodding, she rose, shook his hand and left.

Outside, the sky was gray with clouds building along the mountain range. The weatherman had forecasted snow for the afternoon. Maybe he was right for a change. Snow would make it seem more like Christmas.

Cool air brushed against her cheeks, and she moved down the sidewalk toward the truck she'd borrowed from her parents. She greeted friends as she passed them, but Isaac's words echoed in her head.

She'd made an offer to Holly Johnson, which wasn't as much as Bryg had offered, but Holly had agreed because she wanted the land to be preserved. She'd have to tell Holly and her parents she couldn't buy the ranches now, but she'd think of a way.

That wouldn't help Holly. The older woman couldn't work her ranch much longer. Leah couldn't forget how tired Holly had looked when Leah had brought the boys to church for the pageant rehearsal. She couldn't call Holly. She had to be honest and up front with her friend.

If Leah couldn't buy the Johnson ranch, what would Holly do? Leah felt wretched. The older woman was ready to retire. Unless Leah found a way to buy the ranches, Holly would sell to someone else … like Bryg.

Snow fell, the flakes big and wet, and Leah rushed to the truck. Should she wait until after Christmas and see if she could figure out a way to buy the ranches, or should she call Bryg, tell him she couldn't buy the ranches, and ask him if his offer were still good?

Or she could find another buyer, someone who wanted to buy a ranch and keep it as a ranch. How hard would that be? Maybe the ministry that had offered to send a couple to raise the foster boys knew someone who could buy the ranch *and* raise foster children.

Heavy snow clung to Leah's hair when she climbed into the truck and turned on the engine. She dialed Holly's phone number, but it rang to voicemail. Leah glanced at the clock on the dashboard. Tonight was the Christmas pageant. Holly was probably at church getting everything set up.

Leah had told her parents she'd take the boys to the church and help them get ready so her parents had a moment to relax. When she took the boys to church, she'd find a moment when she and Holly could talk. In the meantime, Leah would find a way to make her plan work.

LEAH PARKED the van in front of the church. The boys talked and laughed and leaped out of the van. Even Zeke was excited about his role as a shepherd in the pageant. Leah often heard him in his room reciting his lines.

Inside the church, the boys called to their friends and thundered down the stairs to change into their costumes. Leah followed.

In the center of the large room, Holly helped shepherds and angels slip into robes and adjust headpieces. She looked at Leah, the corner of her mouth curving.

Leah took a deep breath.

"You don't have to say anything," Holly said softly. "I already heard."

Leah's eyes went wide. She'd forgotten how quickly word spread in a small town—not that different from the campus. Hadn't half the faculty known she'd broken her engagement with Charlie even before she'd thrown a suitcase into the back of the taxi and headed for the airport?

"I'm so sorry," Leah murmured.

"We tried," Holly said on a rough exhale. "I called the broker, and he already found someone who wants to buy it." Her mouth tipped, and Leah knew then what had happened. Bryg still wanted Holly's ranch.

Leah had tried so hard to make sure the ranch land would be preserved. She had challenged a billionaire. She hadn't lost yet, but it didn't look good.

"In fact …" Holly looked past Leah to the practice room entrance.

Leah looked over her shoulder to Bryg. Her heart was a hot stone plunging through her chest.

When the boys saw Bryg, their surprise turned to barely contained delight, and they raced to him, except Zeke, who tossed his hair, even though it was too short to fall across his face. Hands in his pockets, he sauntered across the room and stood behind the others. He smiled at Bryg, who tapped his shoulder with a closed fist. Bryg said something Leah couldn't hear with all the noise filling the room. It made Zeke laugh and drop his gaze.

Leah's chest squeezed. The boys liked Bryg. In fact, everyone in town seemed to. Several people chatted with him, and he showed genuine interest in whatever they said.

Leah turned back to Holly and saw the older woman watched her.

"I'm glad Bryg is still interested in buying your ranch," Leah said and tried to keep her voice steady. Maybe Bryg was still interested in her parents' ranch, too. Knowing they could retire and get the rest they needed would make it easier for her when she returned to Braxton. Whatever God's plan for Mardale, she'd accept it.

"This will all work out," Holly smiled at her.

The lights in the room flickered, announcing the start of the pageant.

"I better get my shepherds and angels lined up for the performance," Holly said and glanced at the ceiling. A boy tangled in his robe rushed to her, and she unwrapped the mantle from around his shoulders.

"I'll get my boys," Leah said. Getting the boys meant she'd have to talk to Bryg. She released a slow breath. May as well face the music.

The boys, flushed with excitement, talked at once, making sure Bryg knew what they'd been doing, and what they'd accomplished. Bryg listened, his face intense with interest. When Leah approached, he looked at her, and his mouth curved. At least, he didn't seem angry with her. The boys turned to her.

"This is your cue, guys." Leah adjusted Frankie's robe, then Harry's. "Everyone ready?"

They shouted at once, and Leah told them to line up with the other shepherds. They elbowed each other and rushed to the back staircase that led to the altar.

"Thanks for coming," Leah said to Bryg. "The boys are glad you're here."

"What about you?" he asked, his voice low but clear. His gaze felt as if it brushed against her skin.

"I'm glad you came," she stammered and set her jaw. They may be rivals when it came to the future of the valley, but weren't they also friends? She remembered the night in the barn, when they'd been so close. Her walls went up. It was best if she and Bryg were just friends. "Would you like to sit with us?"

"Yes, I would," he said.

She turned away and saw they were the only ones left in the practice room. She looked over her shoulder at him, "We'd better hurry."

"Leah." His voice made her still.

She didn't speak. Slowly, she turned to him.

"I'm sorry your plans to buy Holly's ranch and your parents' ranch didn't go through," he said, the sincerity in his tone giving her a little comfort.

"I can't give up hope that there's still a way to make it work," she said on a rough exhale," but I haven't thought of anything yet."

"That's what I like about you," he said with a soft laugh. "Determined to the end."

"Or too stubborn to know when to quit." She smiled slightly. Maybe this was the lesson she needed to learn—that God knew what He was doing.

The lights in the room flickered again announcing the final seating call.

"I guess we'd better hurry," Bryg said, his voice husky. He extended his hand, indicating he'd follow her up the stairs.

People packed the sanctuary as guests from neighboring towns always attended the Christmas pageant. Bryg greeted several people, which made Leah smile. In the short time he'd been here, he'd made a lot of friends.

Leah looked over the sanctuary and saw her parents standing in a pew and chatting with a couple surrounded by three children. Her mother looked up when Leah and Bryg entered the sanctuary and waved to them.

"I see Mom and Dad." Leah nodded toward her parents. "We can sit with them," she said and moved down the aisle.

Leah greeted the couple talking to her parents and introduced Bryg to them. They were aware of the changes he'd make to the community and were interested in his plans.

Leah listened as Bryg explained his ideas. She tried not to think of what the development would mean to the meadows where she'd ridden her horses. Everything was part of God's plan. She wouldn't be in Mardale after the holiday. She'd return to Braxton. What happened after she left shouldn't matter.

Something hot filled her chest. Whatever happened in Mardale would always matter.

The pastor stepped to the podium. The lights dimmed. Everyone grew quiet, and the pastor opened the pageant with a prayer.

A young man's voice, Frankie's voice, sang the opening song. Leah trembled slightly at the words that promised hope and peace. She felt Bryg's gaze and looked at him. His brow lifted in question. She gave him a reassuring smile, but couldn't ignore the warmth and tenderness she felt whenever he was near. For a moment, she wondered what it would be like to always feel his presence.

She pushed that thought from her mind. Why was she thinking anything about Bryg? Before the holidays, she had to return to campus for two weeks, then she'd return to Mardale Christmas Eve and stay until the winter quarter started. This Christmas break would be her last chance to see the valley in its pristine state. After the construction started, it would be difficult to return to Mardale.

The tension building in her chest almost made it hard to breathe. She tried to relax. She was here to enjoy the pageant, not think about Bryg's plans for the community she loved.

She lifted her gaze to the shepherds. Her parents' boys strolled onto the stage. The robes didn't hide the tough personas they had formed in the homes where their tenuous lives had begun, but their performances spellbound the audience. Leah wondered if the shepherds who had visited the Christ child had been tough men.

She glanced at Bryg and saw his gaze riveted to the stage. As if he felt her look at him, he shifted his eyes to hers. The smile spreading over his face made her heart warm. What lucky woman would see that for the rest of her life? Why wasn't he seeing someone now? Every picture of him on the internet showed him with a different woman.

With a start, Leah realized who Bryg wasn't—he wasn't the man the media portrayed, the man she had assumed he was. On the websites, he was portrayed as a jet-setter.

Leah flushed at her preconceived notions. She'd never given Bryg a chance. She'd made up her mind about him and didn't even know him.

Bryg Winslow was warm and caring and concerned. How many times had he reworked the development to make sure it met with her parents' approval?

And her approval. She wouldn't live here, yet he'd taken her opinions into account.

The cast singing the final song brought Leah's face up. When the song ended, the cast spread across the stage. The sanctuary lights grew brighter, and the cast bowed. The audience stood and applauded.

Bryg stood next to Leah, and she glanced at him. When she saw his admiration for the performance shining in his eyes, her heart squeezed tight. Would he ever marry and have a family? If he did, he'd be a wonderful father. She remembered how he played ball with the boys. He had the energy to keep up with them. She released a slow breath. She wouldn't think about Bryg's future. She wouldn't be part of it, so Bryg's life shouldn't matter to her.

The applause faded, and the performers dashed down the stage to greet family and friends. The boys raced through the crowds to Leah, her parents and Bryg.

"You were fabulous." Leah hugged each boy whose eyes brightened at the praise.

Her parents and Bryg echoed the admiration. They moved downstairs with other audience members to an open area set up with tables laden with punch and cookies. The boys were too excited to eat and dashed around the room with their friends. Frankie stood in one group, the pretty girl Leah had seen talking to him before at his side. Leah's heart sighed at the look of young love—not that she was old, but looking at Frankie and the girl made her feel ancient.

Even Zeke stood with a group of guys. Leah smiled when she saw him check out a girl across the room. The girl shyly showed her interest in him, and who wouldn't? With his dark eyes and his powerful build, Leah was surprised only one girl showed interest in him.

When Leah turned back to the conversation, she noticed Bryg watching her. He looked past her to Zeke and then looked at the girl. He smiled. Did he remember the time when he'd first noticed girls? She shoved the wistful thought from her mind and hoped those girls realized how lucky they'd been to catch the eye of Bryg Winslow.

The surrounding conversations lessened, and Leah noticed families bidding friends goodbye and walking up the stairs.

"I'll get the boys," Leah said to her parents.

The boys had calmed from their post-performance excitement.

Harry and Carl looked like they were ready to drop from exhaustion. They all talked at once as Leah, her parents and Bryg guided them up the stairs.

Bryg walked out of the church with them.

"Are you coming by the house?" Zeke asked him.

"Well," Bryg said slowly. His gaze moved from Leah's parents to Leah.

"You're welcome to stop by." Leah glanced at her parents and saw that they'd like it if he did.

"I have room in my car, if you want me to take a few passengers," Bryg said.

"I want to go." Frankie stepped forward. The other boys chimed in—including Zeke.

"If it's okay with Vern and Mavis, it's okay with me," Bryg said.

The boys jerked their gazes to Leah's parents, who nodded their consent. Shouts rose above the group, and they dashed across the parking lot to Bryg's SUV.

"I was going to ask you to come, too." He looked at Leah.

A soft smile teased the corner of his lips, and she tried to slow her ricocheting pulse.

"I'll meet you at the house," she said. Amazing how calm she sounded.

Bryg followed Leah's parents' van to the ranch and parked in the gravel circle in front of the house. The boys piled out, exhaustion evident in their movements when they thanked Bryg for the ride, walked into the house and up the stairs to their rooms.

"Thanks for giving them a ride and for coming to the performance tonight," Leah murmured when the others had gone inside.

"I was glad to give them a ride, and as for coming tonight, I wouldn't have missed it." His voice soft, he looked straight at her. "What are your plans?"

"I'll do what I had originally planned to do." She gave a dry laugh. "I'll fly back to Braxton and tie up a few loose ends." Namely, talk to Charlie——she couldn't put that off any longer. She wanted to have a plan to buy her parents' ranch and Holly's ranch, but she had to trust God. What was His plan? "But I'll be back for the holidays."

Would Bryg? She wouldn't ask him. If the answer were no, it would break the boys' hearts … to say nothing of hers. But why would he want to come back after the wrench she'd thrown in his plans? Yet, he'd come to the pageant tonight, much to the boys' relief.

Face it. It was for your relief, too.

When she returned to the ranch, it would be different than in previous years. Bryg could've started his development on Holly's ranch. Could she stand seeing bulldozers and survey stakes impaled across the beautiful meadows? She swallowed and tried to quiet the emotions that tangled around her heart.

"I wish you'd trust me on this project," Bryg said, his eyes filled with an intensity that made her breath catch. He took her hand. The warmth in his touch flooded her.

Air rushed from her lungs. Never had a man's touch felt like this. Confusion gripped her. For a moment, she could almost believe that his look was more than wanting her approval for the development.

She needed to clear her head. Being this close to Bryg sent her thoughts into a tailspin. She stepped from him. His hand fell away, and she tightened her jaw against the cool air stealing his warmth. Bryg would develop Mardale, and then he'd leave. Her heart ached to make room for this dynamic man who showed care and concern for others.

She could tell Bryg cared about her, but for how long? She had thought Charlie had cared for her, and maybe he had in the beginning.

Her throat closed. She hadn't guarded her heart against Charlie because she hadn't realized how painful love could be. Now she knew. Never again would she drop her guard. And if she never married?

That gave her a start, but she had her career. It didn't keep her warm at night, but the accolades she received almost made up for a life of knowing a man loved her and that she had children who loved her.

Almost.

"What is it, Leah?" Bryg's voice was hoarse, his gaze intense.

"What do you mean?" Frowning, she shook her head. She was careful. She knew she hadn't given anything away.

"Whenever we're close, you pull away—as if you can't trust me." He didn't move closer, but he seemed closer.

She took a step back. "I don't think I'm pulling away." If she weren't pulling away, why had she put distance between her and Bryg?

His mouth flattened. His gaze narrowed. He didn't believe a word she'd said.

Neither did she.

"My mistake," he murmured.

Leah's heart thrashed inside her chest. Pressure built within her. Why hadn't she told him the truth? He knew she didn't want the town to change. He'd had his staff redesign the development three times. Each modification was better than the last, and the first had been perfect.

But how did she confess that she wasn't ready to let the town of Mardale go? She definitely couldn't let her heart go. Christmas Eve was supposed to be her wedding day.

She tried to still the ache in her heart. She wasn't sad she and Charlie wouldn't get married. She was sad she wouldn't *be* married. She was ready—ready to start a family. If she hadn't walked in on Charlie and his assistant, she and Charlie would marry in two weeks. She would've made a terrible mistake.

Slowly, so slowly, Bryg reached for her hand and tugged her to him.

She didn't pull away, and her heart fell. She loved the warmth and feeling in his touch. Even if for a moment, she wanted to be close to this powerful and compassionate man. Canceling her engagement to Charlie had toughened her. When she and Bryg went their separate ways, she wouldn't hurt as much as she had when she'd set her engagement ring on Charlie's bookcase and walked out of his office while he and his assistant sat frozen and stared after her.

"I don't know what happened, and I'm sorry someone could be so callous to damage your heart." Bryg's voice was rough with emotion.

He set his hands on her shoulders. "But I hope someday, when you aren't afraid to heal, you'll call me, and let me know you're ready. Promise me that."

Leah stared at him, stunned. How could Bryg be so in tune with the turmoil churning inside her? He was Bryg Winslow. He ran a multi-billion-dollar corporation. In a week, he'd be so caught up in another development, it might take him awhile to remember who she was.

"If you're thinking I won't remember who you are, you'd be wrong." Lowering his head, he pressed his lips to her forehead. The touch was warm, soft and filled with compassion. His lips lingered a moment, then he stepped back. His hands slowly slid away from her shoulders.

The kiss was like an electrical current bouncing from her toes to the crown of her head. She looked at him and tried to draw air into her lungs.

"Goodnight, Leah," Bryg said. Turning away, he walked to his SUV. At the driver's door, he hesitated and looked back at her.

Make him that promise. The day you're ready, you'll tell him. The voice inside her head pounded like a war drum.

She couldn't. She couldn't give her heart to someone else, especially someone as powerful as Bryg, because at that moment, she knew the pain she'd feel when he walked away, would send her to her knees.

BRYG LOOKED in his rearview mirror when he drove away from the Rendell ranch house. Leah still stood in the gravel circle and watched after him.

His chest squeezed when he turned the corner and couldn't see her anymore. Would he see her again? Probably. She'd come home for Christmas and he'd be here overseeing the development. He hadn't planned to be, but now he'd make sure he was.

He knew when he saw Leah again, their moments together would be strained. He wanted to reach her, but the wall she'd built around her heart strengthened every time he tried.

His entire life he'd faced challenges. Nothing appealed to him more than someone telling him no, a word that had never been in his vocabulary. Very little stopped him. When he felt a deal slipping through his fingers, he worked hard to keep it. He'd lost a few, but not recently.

Until now.

Leah was slipping through his fingers. Every time he closed his eyes, he saw her—her thick, dark curls spilling over her shoulders, her golden eyes alive and vibrant, especially when making a point. The curve of her neck when she tipped her head. The subtle fragrance of her skin that made him want to pull her into his arms and taste her full, soft lips.

That she spoke her mind made him want to be near her even more. She had what few women he'd met had—a toughness that didn't hide her femininity. Leah Rendell was all woman and a caring woman. Her inner beauty had drawn him to her. He wasn't ready to let her go, but in her eyes he saw the fortress was in place. It would take an army to bring it down.

He tapped his closed fist against the steering wheel. His mouth tight, he drove down the country road. What man had damaged Leah so she couldn't trust? If Bryg ever met the guy, it would be hard for him not to want to take a swing at him. Bryg may have left the streets, but the streets hadn't left him. As a kid, he'd learned to defend himself. He made sure he never lost a fight. He doubted the man who'd hurt Leah would know what to do if he and Bryg ever faced each other.

Bryg took a breath, filling his lungs and pressing them against his heart, something he'd learned to do as a kid whenever someone bigger threatened him. He won those battles by keeping a cool head.

That was the only way to Leah's heart. It had to be her decision. She had to be ready to make that choice. What would that decision be? To walk away?

He released a slow breath. Whatever she decided, he'd have to accept it.

CHAPTER 13

*L*eah settled into the plane's seat and stared out the window.

Christmas Eve. The day that should've been her wedding day. She felt empty, and she felt cold. Not because Charlie broke her heart. He had, and she hadn't healed completely, but God's grace gently moved her in the right direction.

A month ago, she had planned for a completely different Christmas Eve—a day when she would've walked down the aisle overflowing with joy because her future husband waited for her at the altar. Somehow, she made it through the last two weeks when she left Mardale and returned to Braxton to tie up loose ends before the winter quarter. She didn't discuss teaching remotely with the dean, because she wouldn't stay in Mardale. For now, Braxton was her home.

When she returned to her condo, the phone was ringing. Charlie's number appeared on her caller ID. She wondered if he'd called every day, hoping she'd pick up the phone.

She and Charlie had spoken once while she was in Mardale. His apology was heartfelt, but when he asked if they could start over, she had said it would be better for both of them if they went their separate ways. Charlie hadn't agreed and had asked her to reconsider. She told him she already had.

The phone stopped ringing. Tension eased from Leah's chest. She'd use her time in Braxton to focus on her next quarter's classes and trust God that the changes Bryg would make in her hometown were part of His plan.

The phone rang again. She released a soft exhale. She couldn't avoid Charlie. She'd hear what he had to say.

She answered the phone. When Charlie started to apologize for the umpteenth time, she told him he didn't have to, and then she realized how freeing forgiveness could be.

She was ready to move on with her life. She wished him the best with his.

"Is there someone else?" Charlie asked.

That made her breath catch. The image of Bryg looking at her with such concern in his eyes filled her with unfamiliar emotions. She couldn't have these feelings for Bryg. There was nothing between them.

She walked to the picture window that overlooked the town's square.

"Leah, are you there?" Charlie asked.

"I'm here, and no, there's no one else," she said, her voice quiet and controlled. She closed her eyes. Bryg wasn't part of her life. She'd closed that door firmly.

She was so calm when she ended the call, it took her a moment to realize what she hadn't done—she hadn't cried. The knot in her stomach slowly unwound.

Charlie had done her a favor. She could've made the biggest mistake of her life, but thanks to her perfect timing——when she caught him with his assistant——Leah learned Charlie wasn't the man for her.

The two weeks she'd spent in Braxton helped get her mind off the changes Bryg planned for Mardale and focus on her life in Braxton. She didn't live in Mardale anymore. The final decision for Bryg's changes should be made by those who did.

Leah stared out the plane's window while the airline captain reported the weather in Denver, and the plane's arrival time. A bubble of joy wrapped around her heart. She was on her way to Mardale to spend Christmas with her parents and the boys. That was the greatest Christmas gift of all.

When Leah arrived in Denver, her mother met her at the airport with the truck. Leah said little on the drive back to the ranch. As they neared Holly's old ranch, Leah's heart rate picked up speed. Bryg had bought the Johnson property. Had he started the development? What changes would she see when she and her mother drove home?

When the truck crested the hill, Leah looked over the valley to Holly's old ranch. The valley looked as it had when she'd left. There were no plowed fields and no stakes with orange flags dotting the countryside. Leah released a shaky breath.

"Bryg won't start work until we've finished raising the boys," her mother said, giving Leah a start.

She gave a soft laugh. Her mother had always been good at reading her mind. "Do you know why?"

"He didn't say, but I'm assuming he has some things to finalize." Her mother gripped the steering wheel with both hands. When she glanced at Leah, there was relief in her face.

Leah felt relief, too.

At the house, Leah carried her suitcase inside. The boys sat around the dining room table and worked on a school project with her father, who stood and hugged her. The boys jumped up from the table and greeted her before her father guided them back to the project.

The house looked and smelled like Christmas, which filled Leah with the joy she'd felt from her childhood. She hadn't decorated her condo, because she knew she wouldn't spend Christmas there. After unpacking and changing into jeans and a sweater, she helped her mother in the kitchen. She lifted the lid on the slow cooker and inhaled the rich aroma of roasted chicken and vegetables, but her mind was elsewhere. What were Bryg's plans?

"If you want to know what's going on, go to the old Johnson ranch and see for yourself." Her mother looked at her.

"Is Bryg there?" Leah asked, her heart drumming a steady beat. She couldn't avoid him forever. Mardale was small, and she and Bryg were bound to meet, but he ran an empire. He may not even be at the ranch.

"I don't think so," her mother said, and that made Leah breathe a little easier. "There's always someone in town who knows when his jet flies into the community airport, and no one has said anything. You know he lives at the Johnson's old ranch house."

"No, I didn't know that." Leah's head came up.

"I thought I told you." Her mother frowned. "Anyway, when he's in town, he stays there, which was a relief to know it wouldn't sit abandoned during the development. He drives by, whenever he's here. If any of us is outside, he always stops and chats, which thrills the boys. Drive over to the old Johnson ranch. See what he's done."

"Have you seen it?" A bubble of panic welled in her stomach.

"From the road. I'm always in a rush to get the boys somewhere," her mother said, and Leah pressed her lips together. This was another reason her parents should retire. "But you can go."

"I will later." Leah lowered the slow cooker's lid.

"Go now." Her mother waved her away from the counter. She lifted an eyebrow at her. "You can drive the truck."

"Thanks," Leah murmured, and walked out of the kitchen. Her mother was right. Until she saw what Bryg had done, her curiosity would torture her.

Fifteen minutes later, she guided the truck down the gravel driveway that led to Holly's house—Bryg's house.

Bryg stood in the front yard, an ax in hand. A log stood in the center of an old tree stump——the one Holly's husband had used to chop kindling. Bryg swung the ax over his head, the muscles in his back swelling and filling out his sweater. With a clean sweep, the ax sliced the log into two pieces.

Leah stopped the truck at the driveway entrance. Her heart leaped. Bryg hadn't looked up, so maybe he hadn't heard her drive in. If she backed out of the driveway now, he wouldn't know she'd come.

He looked over his shoulder. Seeing her, he turned, a smile

pressing thumbprint dimples into his firm jaw. Her stomach quivered. His pleasure at seeing her couldn't have been more apparent.

She drove the length of the driveway and stopped a few feet from him. He didn't approach the truck, just watched her. She waited a moment and then climbed out. They weren't in high school, and she wasn't the shy girl who blushed whenever she talked to a guy. Okay, she still blushed, but she was a college professor. She should act like one.

Bryg remained still, his eyes never leaving her.

"Hello," she said. She slipped fingers into the front pocket of her jeans and stepped toward him.

"Hello, Leah. It's good to see you," he said, his voice husky. He watched her every move. The light in his eyes was like a caress against her cheek, and she remembered the night he'd kissed her forehead. A tremble moved across her shoulders, making her take a deep breath.

"It's good to see you, too," she murmured. She dropped her gaze before she stood there and gawked at him.

"I take it you just flew in," he said. Feeling him look at her was distinctly unsettling.

"Yes, Mom said …" She stopped. She wouldn't blame her mother for her spontaneous visit. "I wanted to see what you've done to the place."

"By all means." He smiled and waved a hand toward the ranch house that looked as it did when Holly had lived there. He looked back at her.

"You haven't done anything yet," she said, confused

He gave a soft laugh. "No, I've decided I like it the way it is."

"You're not going to change anything?" Leah blinked. Her heart picked up speed. Was he going to make changes at her parents' place instead? Her throat went dry. He'd tear down the house where she'd been raised, along with the barn, the pigpen, the work sheds.

"Leah, don't look like that," Bryg said, his voice soft. His mouth tipped into a hesitant smile.

"Like what?" Her face came up.

"Like a deer caught in the headlights," he said. "I'm not saving the big project for your parents' place."

Leah stood rooted in shock. How well did Bryg know her? Apparently, enough to know her thoughts.

"Then where will you start the big project?" She narrowed her eyes at him. What other ranch had he bought, and why hadn't her parents told her?

"I've started here." He tipped his head toward the house. "Come inside. I'll show you."

Leah didn't know if she could stomach the changes he would've made. The Johnson house had lead glass transoms and knotty pine flooring. The old kitchen appliances had been Leah's favorite feature in the house.

Bryg swept his hand toward the front porch, indicating she should lead the way.

She walked up the front steps and went inside. She squinted until her eyes grew accustomed to the dim lighting. The antiques that had filled the Johnson home were gone. Holly would've taken those when she moved. The furniture filling the entry looked normal, as if a family lived there, and it wasn't the chrome and glass furnishings decorators stashed inside a bachelor pad. In the living room, an arrangement of comfortable looking armchairs, sofa and loveseat surrounded the fireplace. A Christmas tree sat in an alcove of bay windows. In the dining room across the hall sat a table, chairs and breakfront.

Frowning, she looked at him. "You have a Christmas tree," she said slowly.

"It is Christmas." His mouth tipped in a way that made her laugh.

"Other than the new furniture, I don't see any changes."

"I didn't make any." When she frowned at him, he said, "I'm not going to." She opened her mouth, and he held up his hand. "There's been a change in plans."

Leah didn't like the sound of that. Her hands shook, and she balled them into fists.

"Do you want a drink of water?" He frowned and looked genuinely concerned.

She started to shake her head, then nodded. She couldn't speak.

He pushed into the kitchen and appeared a moment later with a glass. Taking her hand, he led her through the glass pocket doors and into the living room. When she sat, he handed her the glass and sat in the chair opposite her. His elbows on his knees, he dropped his hands between his legs and lifted his gaze to hers.

Her heart thrashed inside her chest as she waited for him to say something she knew she wouldn't want to hear.

"I'm not going through with the development." He looked straight into her eyes as if to gauge her reaction.

The glass slipped slightly in Leah's hand, and she gripped it hard. He frowned. Removing the glass from her hand, he set it on an end table.

"Maybe we should discuss this another time," he said. The corner of his mouth tipped.

"No, I'd like to hear about your 'change in plans.'" Why was she being so emotional about land? The ranch had always been important to her, but then Bryg came along, and with him came new ideas and changes. "Did you sell the development to someone else?" She sounded panicky, and she winced. She needed to let Bryg explain.

"No," he said. "I still own the Johnson Ranch, and I've no intention of selling it. I'll close on your parents' ranch when they're ready."

"I don't understand." She shook her head.

"At first, I didn't either." He gave a dry laugh. " The more I worked on the development, the more I realized this wasn't what I wanted."

"But the community." A shiver of alarm raced along her nerve endings.

She had fought him every step of the way. Now, he was stepping back, abandoning the development, leaving Mardale intact. He was giving her what she wanted.

And what of the community? The population had dropped over the past thirty years. The development would've enticed families to move to a dying town. Without it, people wouldn't have a reason to move to the area, which meant the land values would drop.

"Before you start running all those scenarios through your mind, let me tell you what my next plan is," he said. "I'm working on a campaign to attract a younger generation of ranchers and farmers to the area. I've already set up a team to reach out to people working in big cities with the offer they telecommute and continue in their jobs while working the land or raising horses or cattle or even pigs. Whatever they want."

"Is that what you're going to do?" Her eyes widened.

It was nice that he'd moved into Holly's house and kept it as a home, but the house was no Manhattan penthouse. Mardale wasn't Manhattan. He'd miss the energy of the big city.

"I have something else in mind for myself." He looked at her as if he knew she was judging him.

Her cheeks burned. Hadn't she judged him from the moment she'd met him? She'd never given him a chance, and he'd been kind to her. She remained silent. She'd stuck her foot in her mouth so many times it was beginning to hang open.

"I want to take over your parents' foster home." Bryg looked straight into Leah's eyes.

She blinked. She knew she hadn't heard him correctly.

"You know what my life was like before the Moores took me in," he said on an exhaled breath. "I didn't know my father. My mother abandoned me when I was young. I learned later she died." Emotion filled his throat, and he waited a moment.

The pain in his eyes scooped air from Leah's lungs. Silently, she wished he hadn't suffered as a child, but that had been the life that made him Bryg Winslow.

"Stories about my past are all over the internet. Some of it true, a lot made up. I gave up a long time ago trying to correct the fabrications. People can think what they want," he said. "One thing I never forgot was how kind the Moores had been to me. When I started making money, I tried to repay them for what they'd done, but they wouldn't accept anything. They helped me and other children because it was their calling." His expression revealed something much deeper than appreciation. "The first time I stepped into your family's home and saw what your parents were doing for those four boys, I realized that was my calling, too. It took me awhile to accept that, but I realized that no matter how much money I made, it was never enough to separate me from my past. I had a tough life, but it made me who I am. I have the means to help others. I'm ready to do that now." He looked at her and leaned back in his chair.

"I owe you an apology." Leah could barely utter the words. She dropped her gaze to her hands clasped tightly in her lap. She'd made up her mind who Bryg Winslow was, and she'd been wrong ... so wrong. Wrong to assume he only wanted to make money, and wrong to assume he was like Charlie.

He was nothing like Charlie.

"You don't owe me anything." Bryg took her hand.

Warmth radiated through her. She swallowed and tried to calm the turmoil of emotions rising up her throat. The touch was gentle and caring, and it felt so right to have his sinewy hand wrapped around hers.

"But there's something else I have to say." He looked at her. "I can't stop thinking about you, Leah. I think I first realized I loved you when Babe escaped the pigpen. I hadn't known a woman could be so compassionate, but I feel it whenever I'm near you. I love you, Leah."

"Love?" Leah's mouth trembled.

"Yes, love." He exhaled slowly. "I know you've been hurt. I don't know who hurt you, and I don't need to. What I want you to understand is that I'm not that man. I can wait for as long as it takes for you to give me a chance. All I want to know is that I have a chance."

She laughed softly and dropped her gaze. "Falling in love with you was the last thing I wanted to do, especially after ..." She looked into his dazzling blue eyes. "I kept telling myself it wasn't possible that I love you."

"What do you tell yourself now?" He looked at her, his heart in his hands.

Her lips parted. Never had a man looked at her with such love in his eyes. Bryg loved her for herself, not how she could boost his career.

"That I can't fight this feeling anymore," she said, her voice husky.

"That's all I needed to know." He tugged her hand, pulling her to him.

He slipped an arm beneath her legs. His strength scooped air from her lungs when he lifted her to his lap. He pushed his nose into her hair and inhaled deeply.

She settled her head against the ridged muscles of his chest. Through his sweater, she felt his heart pick up speed. She closed her eyes. She loved the warmth of him, the scent of him, the feeling of his powerful arms wrapped around her.

"Whenever you're ready, I'd like to make this permanent," he said, his voice rumbling through his chest. When she lifted her gaze to his, he said, "I'll be ready any time. I don't want to rush you."

"You're not rushing me," she said. Her heart melted. "I'll need to talk to the college to see what can be arranged about my classes."

He released a slow breath. "That's all I needed to know." He rose and set her on her feet. Bowing to one knee, he took her hand. "Leah Rendell, will you marry me?"

"Yes, yes, yes," she murmured, her voice filled with emotion.

"You've made me happier than I ever thought possible." Rising to his feet, he took her in his arms. He lowered his face to hers, his lips touching hers tenderly and gently and with a passion she'd never felt before. "You've just given me the best Christmas gift I could ever imagine," he said against her lips.

She opened her eyes and looked into his. "To say nothing of what you've given me."

When she looked past him, she looked out the picture window that faced the front yard. A blanket of snow fell past the window.

Bryg frowned, then turned to the window.

Taking his hand, she led him to the window. "It's beautiful," she whispered.

"Like you," he said with feeling.

The sincerity in his voice could almost make her believe she was.

Bryg glanced at the ceiling. Her gaze followed his—to a sprig of mistletoe dangling from the ceiling. She gave a soft gasp.

"We can't break tradition," he said, the corner of his mouth tipping.

"By all means no." She slipped her arms around his neck.

He wrapped his arms around her waist and held her close. His mouth slanting over hers, he kissed her, his love sweeping over her and making her insides quake. How could a kiss be filled with such affection and so much more? She leaned against him and listened to his heartbeat. She had the rest of her life to find out.

EPILOGUE

On a beautiful spring morning, Leah, dressed in a white, beaded gown her mother had made, lifted her gaze to Bryg. Around them sat friends from town and friends they'd known for the last few years——an interesting combination of haute couture and Sunday best. Frankie, Zeke, Harry and Carl stood like stair steps next to Bryg and looked handsome in their new suits. Leah's bridesmaids, friends from high school and college, wore mauve and stood next to her.

Pastor Chuck read the scriptures of love, and Leah tried to pay attention, but when Bryg took her hand, when she felt this powerfully built man's warmth and tenderness, everything around her dissolved. She looked into Bryg's beautiful eyes, her heart floating inside her chest. These would be the eyes she'd look into every morning for the rest of her life.

Her hand quivered in Bryg's sinewy palm. He arched a brow at her, and she gave him a tremulous smile. When he repeated the vows Pastor Chuck recited, tears of joy slid down her face. Her maid of honor peeked around Leah and dabbed her cheeks to spare her makeup, but Leah knew it was a lost cause. Maybe she'd have time to repair her makeup before the photographer took the formal pictures.

Bryg slipped the ring on her finger, and Leah gave a soft gasp. The gold band glistened in the light. The symbol of their love announced to the world that she and Bryg were husband and wife.

Pastor Chuck prayed the final blessing. Leah and Bryg faced their guests, who rose to their feet, their cheers and applause echoing inside Leah's chest.

Ushers from the church replaced the rows of chairs with round tables covered with white tablecloths. The caterers set up the buffet.

The rest of the evening became a blur for Leah. She met Bryg's foster parents, Adam and Cheryl Moore, and greeted other guests. Except for the piece of wedding cake Bryg fed her, she ate nothing. With her shaky stomach, she didn't dare try.

When Bryg slipped an arm around her waist and told her he was taking her home, her pulse beat wildly. Guests lined the sidewalk, tossed rose petals, and called out their good wishes as Leah and Bryg dashed to the SUV decorated with streamers and a "Just Married" sign.

At the house, Bryg swept Leah from the SUV and carried her over the threshold. In the entryway, he set her on her feet. Looking into her eyes, his face softened and his mouth tipped. Lifting his hands to her hair, he removed the pearl studded pins, letting her dark curls tumble to her shoulders.

She couldn't speak. She could only sigh. A deep sound came from his throat. He pushed fingers through her hair, the passion in his touch making her tremble inside. He pressed a kiss to the curve of her neck.

In one swift move, he slipped an arm beneath her knees, pulled her to his chest and climbed the stairs two steps at a time.

SEVEN MONTHS LATER ...

Leah rested a hand on the slight curve of her stomach and took one last look at the table set for the Christmas Eve Celebration with her parents, her brother, David, and his family, the boys and the Moores. The tree glistening in the corner of the living room was piled with colorfully wrapped gifts.

How Leah baked and cooked while fighting the queasiness in her stomach, she didn't know, but she was determined to host the Christmas Eve celebration and couldn't wait to have the family fill the house.

Through the window, Leah watched Bryg set the snow shovel in the corner of the front porch. He stepped into the house, a bluster of snow following him through the front door. He lifted his gaze to hers, his smile pressing dimples into his cheeks that made her heart melt. Each time she looked at him, it was like the first time. She'd never get used to the full lips that kissed her every morning and every night and many times throughout the day.

The past year had brought more changes than she could've imagined. Bryg had proposed to her last Christmas Eve, but it bothered him he hadn't given her an engagement ring.

A few days before she was scheduled to return to the college, Bryg planned to fly her to New York to meet with an exclusive jewelry designer so they could discuss her ring.

Looking into Bryg's eyes, she saw his desire to make her happy, and compassion filled her heart. "I don't need a ring to remind me that you love me," she said and looked into the blue eyes reflecting the affection he expressed to her several times a day.

"I'm not trying to buy your love," he said. "I just want the world to know you're mine."

"*I* know I'm yours," she said with a soft laugh.

"I want to buy you an engagement ring." Taking her hand, he pulled her to him, pressing the length of her body flat against his.

Her head against his chest, she heard his heart thunder beneath the ridged muscles and breathed the subtle hint of his masculine scent.

"Let's go to Henri's on Main Street. He designs his own jewelry. Several of my friends here have bought their rings from his shop." She tipped her face to his and saw the doubt filling his eyes.

"If that's what you want," he said on an exhaled breath.

"I don't want anything, but if a ring will make you feel better, then let's compromise and buy it from Henri."

Bryg had been pleasantly surprised that Henri had won several awards for his designs, and Bryg and Leah decided on a setting that Leah loved and had impressed Bryg.

When Christmas break ended, Leah didn't know how she had the strength to leave Bryg and return to Braxton to teach her winter quarter classes.

When she arrived in Braxton, she scheduled a meeting with the department chair to discuss switching her status to online teaching. The dean had resisted until she presented her letter of resignation. She'd already talked to other universities about teaching online. She didn't want to leave Braxton, but knowing she'd have a position close where filled her with relief. If she left Braxton, a sizeable portion of the college's donor base would leave, and the dean wouldn't let that happen. Her offer was plain——let her teach remotely, or she would tender her resignation.

The dean gave a soft laugh and told her to present her proposal with the classes she would teach. Now she had the best of both worlds ——a teaching position at Braxton and a home with Bryg in Mardale.

On an evening in Braxton when she met friends for dinner, she saw Charlie. The meeting had been awkward, but not painful. When he saw the sparkling diamond on her finger, a lost look flickered in his eyes. She swallowed. Charlie now knew they would go their own ways, and she felt relief that Bryg had insisted she have an engagement ring. When Charlie's brows arched with curiosity, Leah told him she and Bryg planned a spring wedding. He wished her the best.

With Bryg, she had the best.

During winter and spring quarters, Leah spent every evening on the phone with Bryg discussing the wedding, which would be simple, and every weekend in Mardale. She slept little and spent every night staying up late grading papers and planning lessons. Each visit to Mardale was an adventure where Bryg showed her the latest changes he'd made at the ranch. She still couldn't believe he wanted to make Mardale his home. That she and Bryg would raise a family in Mardale made her heart float inside her chest. No degrees or awards could compare to the joy she felt knowing their children would be raised on a ranch.

Bryg hung his coat in the closet, then stepped into the living room and threw a couple of logs on the fire, the muscles in his broad shoulders swelling and easing with his movements. Rising, he brushed his hands together and faced her. His eyes lighted when he saw she watched him.

She blushed. She had every right to stare at her own husband, but felt awkward when he caught her.

"What are you thinking?" Bryg stepped to her and drew her to his chest, the ridged muscles in his powerful arms holding her as if she were the delicate babe she'd soon hold in her own arms. The curve in her stomach pressed against his own flat board abs.

"What a wonderful Christmas this is," she said, and rested her head against his chest. The steady rhythm of his heart making her own heart fill with love for this strongly built and gentle man.

"It is wonderful," he said, his voice deep and filled with emotion. "How are you feeling?" He tipped her face and looked into her eyes.

"Fine," she said. Mostly, she was fine. Today, her stomach had been more queasy, but she'd cooked more today than she had since she'd discovered she was pregnant.

Bryg arched a brow at her.

"Don't worry," she said with a laugh. "I'll be fine."

"Maybe we should've pared the guest list," he said, concern filling his face.

"And miss out on a chance to celebrate the holiday with both our families?" She arched her brows in surprise. "No, thank you. I'm glad your foster parents will be here. I hope they'll play a big part in our baby's life."

"You can count on that." Bryg gave a deep laugh. "They'd still have foster children if they had the energy."

"Then that will give them more time to dote on our children." She grinned.

The sound of tires turning over gravel filtered into the living room. Car doors opened and closed, followed by heavy boots stomping up the front steps. Bryg opened the door. On the porch stood Leah's parents and the Moores. Leah's brother and his family and the boys stood behind them.

Bryg's eyes filled with joy and feeling. He stepped aside, welcoming everyone into the house, then drew his foster parents into his arms. He held them close, clinging to them as he may have done as a boy in desperate need of a home.

Leah collected jackets and hats and led everyone into the living room where an assortment of mixed nuts, cheese spreads and relish trays sat on the end tables and coffee tables.

She and Bryg settled on the loveseat while the others sat in chairs around the crackling fireplace. Small talk included the boys and David's children, and they talked about school and activities and the colleges Zeke and Frankie would attend when they graduated high school in the spring.

"Maybe you have more news to tell us." Mavis sipped the tea Leah had served and looked over her cup at Leah.

Leah's breath caught, and she shifted her gaze to her father and then to the others in the room.

"I thought there was a glow about you," Cheryl Moore said with a smile.

Bryg slipped his hand around Leah's, his smile soft and filled with love. The boys and David's children quieted as they realized Bryg and Leah would welcome a little one into their home.

"The baby is due in early May," Bryg said.

"Spring is perfect timing," Mavis said softly, delight shining in her eyes.

"Cool," Zeke said. He grinned and leaned into his chair. "I'll still be here. I'll get to see him."

Everyone laughed.

"Anyone hungry?" Bryg rose, bringing Leah with him.

"Yes." The boys and David's children talked at once. They were on their feet and cast longing looks toward the dining room.

"Good." Leah gestured everyone toward the dining room. "Everyone take a seat."

The boys and David's children were out of the room and pacing around the dining room table when they noticed the placards. They slipped into their chairs.

Leah smoothed a hand over her stomach. A year ago, her life had seemed a shambles when she'd broken her engagement to Charlie and returned home. What was broken, God had made better than new—marriage to a man she had never thought she'd meet. Now, they were expecting their first child.

Bryg's tentative fingers touched hers, then clasped them with the warmth and tenderness so familiar in his touch. His mouth curved slightly with an affection that seemed to grow every day. Never had she thought she'd be blessed with such happiness.

He glanced at the ceiling. Leah's gaze followed his to a sprig of mistletoe.

Her eyes widened. "You put that up?" she whispered.

"Naturally, I can't spend Christmas in this house with my beautiful wife and not have mistletoe." He arched a brow. Bending to her, he gave her a quick kiss.

"I saw that," Frankie shouted and pointed a finger at them.

The corner of Zeke's mouth curved in amusement. The other children made faces.

The adults laughed.

"This is proof we're not going to get away with much once we welcome our new addition," Leah said, and smiled.

"Because that little one will keep us hopping." Bryg gave her hand a gentle squeeze.

He led her to one end of the table. The children watched as he held the chair for her. When Bryg sat at the opposite end of the table, he offered a hand to Carl on his right and one to Zeke on his left. Everyone else fell silent, held hands and bowed their heads.

Bryg's deep voice broke into the quiet with thanksgiving for the meal and blessings for all present.

Leah closed her eyes and soaked in the sound of her husband's voice. Something stirred in her stomach, and she soaked up the warmth filling her.

This life growing inside her was part of her and part of the man who prayed earnestly for everyone present. The love she felt filled her to overflowing, and she breathed deeply to still the emotions tumbling through her chest.

As a child, she never thought she'd leave Mardale. When she left for college, she knew she'd only return for holidays until her parents left.

Now, because of the man who sat at the head of the table, she had a life she never thought possible. In five months, she'd hold the child they created.

Gratitude filled her. The Moores had taken a kid off the street, discovered his strengths and guided him not to be just a financial success, but one who loved the Lord and would be a role model for their children and the other children they'd welcome into their home. She silently offered thanks for the sacrifices the Moores made and what her own parents had given to her and David, to the boys sitting around the table and the ones who had lived in their house over the years.

The four boys here now were on their way to being admirable young men, despite their differences. They had the wisdom to let go of the past and welcome the future. Zeke's acceptance of his new life had been the most welcome victory of all.

Everyone murmured amen and the serving dishes moved around the table. Conversations rose and fell as everyone discussed the joy of the holiday, the new baby, and what the new year would bring.

When they finished dessert, they gathered around the Christmas tree. The boys and David's children barely contained their excitement as they gratefully accepted beautifully wrapped gifts and delighted in the warm jackets and technical gadgets. At the evening's end, Bryg helped everyone pack the gifts into their cars, then he and Leah huddled in their coats on the front porch until the cars disappeared down the driveway.

They stepped into the house now filled with quiet.

"It's too quiet," Leah whispered. Though she was tired, she wished the evening could go on forever. She lifted her gaze to Bryg's brilliant blue eyes filled with love.

"We'll see everyone at your parents' house tomorrow." Bryg's smile reassured her. "Until then, we can celebrate our first Christmas together."

"That's the greatest gift of all." She laid a hand against his chest, felt the beat of his heart.

He slanted his face over hers, his lips tasting her, loving her. He brushed her hair back over her shoulder and trailed kisses down the curve of her neck. He released a ragged breath. "Let's go upstairs," he murmured against the base of her throat.

She took his face between her hands and kissed him, breathed in his subtle scent, then slipped a hand in his. His fingers closed around hers, and she let him lead her up the stairs where she would love and be loved by the man with whom she would share her life for as long as they both shall live.

Merry Christmas, dear Reader!

Start reading The Billionaire's Christmas Promise to find out if Alexander can accept Felicity as his daughter's nanny, or will this angelic woman break past the barriers around his heart and show him the path to love?

DEAR READER

Thank you, Dear Reader, for spending your valuable time reading The Billionaire's Christmas Contract, Book 3 of the Christmas Billionaire Series!

If you enjoyed this book, I would be delighted if you would help me spread the word. You can do this by recommending the book to your friends, to readers' groups and posting comments on discussion boards. You can also tell other readers what you liked about the book through reviews on the site where you purchased the book, or on a reader site such as Goodreads or BookBub.

I love to hear from readers and would be happy to connect with you on twitter @laurarmcneil, on Facebook at facebook.com/ laura-haleymcneil, or by emailing me at laura@ laurahaleymcneil.com.

Would you like to know when my next book is available? You can sign up for my new release email list at www.LauraHaleyMcNeil.com.

Warmest regards.

Laura Haley-McNeil

ABOUT THE AUTHOR

A native of California, Laura Haley-McNeil spent her youth studying ballet and piano, though her favorite pastime was curling up with a good book. Without a clue as to how to write a book, she knew one day she would.

After college, she segued into the corporate world, but she never forgot her love for the arts and served on the board of two community orchestras. Finally realizing that the book she'd dreamt of writing wouldn't write itself, she planted herself in front of her computer. She now immerses herself in the lives and loves of her characters in her romantic suspense and her contemporary romance novels. Many years later, she lived her own romantic novel when she married her piano teacher, the love of her life.

Though she and husband have left warm California for cooler Colorado, they enjoy the outdoor life of hiking, bicycling, horseback riding and snow skiing. They satisfy their love of music by attending concerts and hanging out with their musician friends, but Laura still catches a few free moments when she can sneak off and read.

Laura loves to hear from readers and always responds to emails and letters. If you want to contact Laura, follow the information below.

Sign up for Laura's newsletter at laurahaleymcneil.com.

Email Laura at laura@laurahaleymcneil.com.

Made in the USA
Monee, IL
10 September 2024